Arthur W. Pinero

The Profligate

a play in four acts

Arthur W. Pinero

The Profligate
a play in four acts

ISBN/EAN: 9783337396794

Printed in Europe, USA, Canada, Australia, Japan

Cover: Foto ©Andreas Hilbeck / pixelio.de

More available books at **www.hansebooks.com**

THE PROFLIGATE

A PLAY

In Four Acts

By ARTHUR W. PINERO

"*It is a good and soothfast saw ;*
Half-roasted never will be raw ;
No dough is dried once more to meal,
No crock new-shapen by the wheel ;
You can't turn curds to milk again,
Nor Now, by wishing back to Then ;
And having tasted stolen honey,
You can't buy innocence for money."

LONDON: WILLIAM HEINEMANN

MDCCCXCVIII

INTRODUCTORY NOTE

IT is now more than four years since " The Profligate " was written, and in the interval we have seen many conflicting influences at work upon the theatre, many signs of progress; but in June 1887, although the dramatic atmosphere was full of agitation and uncer-tainty, and the clamorous plaints of the pessimists were loud, the bolt of Norwegian naturalism had not yet fallen upon our stage, Ibsen was still, as far as England was concerned, an exotic of the library. Mr. Pinero, however, appears to have been an unswerving optimist in the face of spreading pessimism ; he evidently felt that the air was clearing, that the period was approaching when the British dramatist might begin to assert his artistic independence, and at least attempt to write plays which should, by means of simple and reasonable dramatic deduction, record actual experience flowing in the natural irregular rhythm of life, which should at the same time embody lofty ideals of conduct and of character. So he wrote " The Profligate," wrote it as he explained, to fit no particular theatrical company, fettered the free develop-ment of his ideas by no exigencies of managerial expediency.

As soon as the play was completed he sought the opinion of one whose attitude towards the drama has always been marked by keen artistic sympathy and generous devotion—that delightful comedian, that masterly manager, John Hare. Mr. Hare's opinion of "The Profligate" found expression in very practical form. He was at that time on the eve of becoming theatrically homeless, but explaining to the author his plans for the future, he begged Mr. Pinero to keep his play for him until such time as he should be in a position to produce it, a request to which Mr. Pinero gladly acceded.

Two years elapsed, during which period the battle of the *isms* had proceeded apace, realism clashing with conventionalism, naturalism with romanticism. And the time now seemed ripe to gauge the practical progress of the modern dramatic movement, as we may call it, to test how far theatrical audiences were really prepared to accept serious drama without "comic relief." The opportunity was at hand, the new Garrick Theatre was completed, and Mr. John Hare produced "The Profligate."

It must be admitted, however, that in doing this a question of managerial policy prompted a concession to popular ·taste or custom which Mr. Pinero had never anticipated in the composition of "The Profligate." He had ended his play with the suicide of the penitent profligate at the very moment that the wife is coming to him with pity and forgiveness in her heart, resolved to share his life again, to bear with him the burden of his past as well as his future—a grimly ironical trick of fate which the author considered to be the legitimate and logical conclusion of this domestic tragedy.

But authors propose, and the "gods" dispose. Mr. Hare, as he frankly admitted in a letter to the papers, felt somewhat timorous of braving the popular prejudice in favour of theatrical happiness in the last act of new plays, and he suggested to Mr. Pinero that, as a matter of expediency, it would be well to alter his *dénouement*, so as to bring about a reconciliation between the reformed profligate and his innocent wife. Mr. Pinero fell in with the managerial views, determining at the same time that, while he allowed the hero of his story to live on with promise of future happiness upon the stage, when the play came to be printed the terrible finality of the tragedy should be restored exactly as it was first written.

Now, therefore, that it has become feasible to place " The Profligate " in the hands of the reader, the author's intention is adhered to, and the play appears in its original form. As a matter of record, however, and for the benefit of those readers who may possibly be interested in comparing the two versions, I think it advisable to append below that portion of the acted text which differs from the play as it is now published, especially since the matter has excited some critical discussion.

The Fourth Act, as generally performed, is entitled "On the Threshold," and the departure from the original occurs on p. 122, when Dunstan Renshaw is about to drink the poison. From that point it runs thus :—

DUNSTAN.

[*He is raising the glass to his lips when he recoils with a cry of horror.*] Ah ! stop, stop ! This is the deepest sin of all my life— blacker than that sin for which I suffer ! No, I'll not ! I'll not ! [*He dashes the glass to the ground.*] God, take my wretched life when You will, but till You lay Your hand upon me, I will live on !

Help me! Give me strength to live on! Help me! Oh, help me!

> [*He falls on his knees, and buries his face in his hands.*
> LESLIE *enters softly, carrying a lamp which she places
> on the sideboard; she then goes to* DUNSTAN.

LESLIE.

Dunstan! Dunstan!

DUNSTAN.

[*Looking wildly at her.*] You! You!

LESLIE.

I have remembered. When we stood together at our prayerless marriage, my heart made promises my lips were not allowed to utter. I will not part from you, Dunstan.

DUNSTAN.

Not—part—from me?

LESLIE.

No.

DUNSTAN

I don't understand you. You—will—not—relent? You cannot forget what I am!

LESLIE.

No. But the burden of the sin you have committed I will bear upon my shoulders, and the little good that is in me shall enter into your heart. We will start life anew—always seeking for the best that we can do, always trying to repair the worst that we have done. [*Stretching out her hand to him.*] Dunstan! [*He approaches her as in a dream.*] Don't fear me! I will be your wife, not your judge. Let us from this moment begin the new life you spoke of.

DUNSTAN.

[*He tremblingly touches her hand as she bursts into tears.*] Wife !
Ah, God bless you ! God bless you, and forgive me !

[*He kneels at her side, she bows her head down to his.*

LESLIE.

Oh, my husband !

This ending found many advocates, even Mr. Clement
Scott and Mr. William Archer, who may be regarded as
representing the opposite poles of dramatic criticism,
agreeing in their decision that this was the only logical
conclusion. "There can be but one end to such a play,"
wrote Mr. Scott, "and Mr. Pinero has chosen the right
one. To make this wretched man whose sin has found
him out a wanderer and an outcast is bad enough ; to
make him a suicide would be worse." Yet there were
others who thought differently.

Wednesday, the 24th of April, 1889, saw the opening
of the Garrick Theatre and the production of "The
Profligate," the programme of which occasion is here
appended.

Programme.

OPENING OF THE GARRICK THEATRE.

THIS EVENING, WEDNESDAY, APRIL 24th, 1889,

WILL BE ACTED

FOR THE FIRST TIME

THE PROFLIGATE

A New and Original Play in Four Acts.

BY

A. W. PINERO.

LORD DANGARS . . .	Mr. JOHN HARE.
DUNSTAN RENSHAW . .	Mr. FORBES ROBERTSON.
HUGH MURRAY . . .	Mr. LEWIS WALLER.
WILFRED BRUDENELL . .	Mr. S. BROUGH.
Mr. CHEAL	Mr. DODSWORTH.
EPHGRAVES	Mr. R. CATHCART.
WEAVER	Mr H. KNIGHT.

Mrs. STONEHAY . . .	Mrs. GASTON MURRAY.
LESLIE BRUDENELL . .	Miss KATE RORKE.
IRENE	Miss BEATRICE LAMB.
JANET	Miss OLGA NETHERSOLE.
PRISCILLA	Miss CALDWELL.

" It is a good and soothfast saw ;
Half-roasted never will be raw ;
No dough is dried once more to meal,
No crock new-shapen by the wheel ; .
You can't turn curds to milk again,
Nor Now, by wishing, back to Then ;
And having tasted stolen honey,
You can't buy innocence for money."

ACT I.

"THIS MAN AND THIS WOMAN."

London; Furnival's Inn;
Mr. MURRAY'S *Room at* Messrs. CHEAL & MURRAY'S.

ACT II.

THE SWORD OF DAMOCLES.

*Florence; On the Road to Fiesole; The Loggia of the Villa
Colobiano.*

ACT III.

THE END OF THE HONEYMOON.

The same place.

ACT IV.

ON THE THRESHOLD.

London; The Old White Hart Hotel, Holborn;
Mr. MURRAY'S *Sitting-Room.*

TIME—THE PRESENT DAY.

The Incidental Song with Guitar Accompaniment, sung by Mr.
AVON SAXON, has been kindly composed by

SIR ARTHUR SULLIVAN.

THE NEW SCENERY PAINTED BY MR. HARFORD.

Probably few who were present on this occasion will need to be reminded of the impression made upon the audience by the new play, or of the plaudits with which it was greeted. The success that attended the initial repre-sentation was echoed for the most part in the chorus of criticism. On all sides the new play was greeted with warm words of welcome, even when these words were qualified by serious critical strictures ; the pessimists regarded it at least as an oasis in the desert of our modern drama, while the optimists hailed it as the herald of a bright new era of English dramatic literature. The various voices of criticism were, in fact, unanimous for once in regarding this as an artistic event of quite unusual importance, even while they were raised to question certain psychological and ethical elements of the play in relation to actual human experience.

It does not come within my province here to discuss the several points of controversy, the various critical objections urged against the play, but merely to recall them as a matter of theatrical history. So be it remem-bered that the central motive of the story was condemned as being fantastically strained, for the simple reason that at this end of the nineteenth century the mental con-dition of Leslie Brudenell was inconceivable, the position therefore being untenable from the point of view of real life. It was further urged that any right-minded young wife would have submissively accepted the situation in the true wisdom of modern cynicism, or that Dunstan Renshaw would have turned round upon her and with brutal frankness revealed to her that her disillusioning was only the common experience of all wives, and that she must bow to the inevitable and make no fuss. It was laid down as law moreover that, as a leopard cannot change its spots, so can no man who has once lived evilly be influenced to a better, a purer life ; that profligate once, profligate he must remain for evermore. Then Hugh Murray, the serious-minded, lofty-natured lawyer, who can never restrain his tongue when he sees wrong-doing, but can be nobly, piteously silent when he must bury his love deep down in his lonely life until it nearly breaks the heart of him—he was found by certain critics to be impossibly unreal and even comic. It was discovered, too, that the office of Messrs. Cheal and Murray was in Furnival's Inn, Fairyland—that such proceedings as were witnessed in that office could never have been possible in Holborn.

Those who made all these discoveries charged "The Profligate" on this score or that with being untrue to nature or false to art. Yet Mr. Pinero, in essaying to deal dramatically with a moral problem in a manner which, while neither cynical nor commonplace, should still be in touch with human sympathy and possible experience, appears to have deliberately set himself to conceive a group of characters, natural yet not ordinary, which should embody his ideals, and with a sufficient sense of actuality evolve the tragic recoil of sin, the dramatic pathos of innocence in contact with the irony of life, the exquisite influence of purity. Whether Mr. Pinero succeeded in carrying out his idea or not, even the severest of his critics could not deny this play respectful consideration. "A real play at last," cried one ; "a faulty play with one faultless act," was another's summing-up after his first enthusiasm had cooled in the refrigerator of time ; while yet a third recorded that "no original English play

produced on our stage for many a day has stirred its
audience so deeply at the time of its representation, or
has sent them home with so much to think over, to
discuss and to remember."

" The Profligate " was performed eighty-six consecu-
tive times at the Garrick Theatre with considerable
success, and, as I believe some impression to the contrary prevails, I may be pardoned for adding, with
results very satisfactory to Mr. Hare's treasury. The
season coming to an end on July 27, the Garrick
closed, and Mr. Hare took " The Profligate " on a brief
provincial tour. At the Prince of Wales's Theatre,
Birmingham, on September 2, it was received with
extraordinary enthusiasm, the local critics poured forth
eulogy upon eulogy, and for the next five nights the house
was crammed. From Birmingham the play went to
Manchester, where it was produced at the Theatre Royal,
on September 9, and performed there nine times. But
the Manchester critics, though respectful in their attitude,
were sparing in their praise. They complained that
Mr. Pinero was neither Dumas nor Augier, compared
him with Georges Ohnet, and found fault with his meta-
phors. And the playgoers of Cottonopolis were depressed,
and bestowed such scant favour upon the play that
Mr. Hare determined to occupy the last three nights of
his engagement with a mirthful adaptation of " Les
Surprises du Divorce," and the Manchester folk then
attended the theatre in their numbers, and laughed, and
were happy again.

A triumph, however, was in store for " The Profligate "
at Liverpool. On September 23, and during the rest of the
week, it was given at the Shakespeare Theatre, and press

and public alike greeted Mr. Pinero's play with acclaim.
Then Mr. Hare returned to town with his company, and
reopened the Garrick with "The Profligate" on Wednesday, October 2. Again was criticism busy with the play,
and the praise of some had cooled, and the praise of
others had warmed, but the original "run" of the play
had been interrupted in the midst of its prosperity, Mr.
Hare had resigned his part to an actor of less influence
and distinction, and after forty-five more performances it
was thought politic to withdraw the play. The notable
fact remains, however, that while theatrical audiences
were still being encouraged to expect "comic relief" and
melodramatic sensation, a serious English drama, which
made no concession to either, had been performed one
hundred and fifty-three times within a few months, with
profit to author and to manager.

But although "The Profligate" had been withdrawn
from the boards of the theatre, its influence was still
active. It commanded a hearing beyond the footlights,
even on the platform of the Literary and Scientific Insti-
tute. Mr. Pinero was invited by the committee of the
Birkbeck Institution to read his play there, and this he
did on the evening of May 16th, 1890, with such marked
success that he has since been invited to repeat the
reading at many of the leading institutions in the
provinces.

But the theatrical career of "The Profligate" was to
take a wider range. The voice of the British dramatist
was to be heard in the land of the foreigner ; but it spoke
in the necessarily mimetic tones of adaptation, and the
tongue was Dutch. "The Profligate," bearing the title
of " De Losbol," was produced in Amsterdam on November

30, 1889, under the personal supervision of Mr J T. Grein, at the Municipal Theatre, which has since been burnt down. Only a partial success is to be recorded, the play having enjoyed but a brief career, as it did also at the Hague, where the production took place at the Royal Theatre. The Dutch critics were for the most part patronising and lukewarm, patronising because the play was English, lukewarm because the author had not treated his theme after the cynical and pessimistic methods of certain modern French writers. But one of the most prominent critics of Holland was fain to admit, in the *Algemeen Handelsblad* of Amsterdam, that "viewed from an English standpoint, 'The Profligate' may certainly be called a remarkable drama," and that "it is a legitimate play with a properly worked-out plot, although it contains a good deal of coincidence, and shows a want of spirit in the dialogue."

"The Profligate" is next heard of in Germany, where "The Magistrate" and "Sweet Lavender" already enjoyed popularity; but there the voice of the author was almost lost in the falsetto tones of the adapter. Dr. Oscar Blumenthal, a well-known German *littérateur* and the popular director of the Lessing Theatre in Berlin, undertook to introduce Mr. Pinero's play to German playgoers. But Dr. Blumenthal has won reputation as a wit and a humorist, and any work from his pen must make his audience laugh before everything ; so he appears to have adopted very drastic measures in preparing "The Profligate" for the German theatre. He has in fact transformed a serious drama of English life into a frivolous comedy of Parisian manners ; innocence is turned into intrigue, the betrayed maiden becomes the scheming adventuress, the play terminates with a laugh, and it is called "Falsche Heilige"—which may be translated as "False Saints." But the result is popular success.

The first performance took place on Friday, February 13, of the present year, at the Stadttheater, Hamburg, and a perfect triumph was achieved, adapter and actors were called before the curtain no less than twenty times, and the press unanimously belauded the "author"—Dr. Blumenthal. Performances then followed with equal success at Altona, Stettin, Graz, München, Dresden, Hildesheim, and Lübeck, and on Saturday, August 29, 1891, "Falsche Heilige" was produced in the German capital at Dr. Blumenthal's own Lessing Theatre. The reception by Berlin playgoers and critics was as enthusiastic as it had been elsewhere, and the glory of the adapter was everywhere. And this is to spread still further, for the play is to visit all the other important theatrical towns of Germany.

This summarises so far the Continental career of "The Profligate," but in all probability it will penetrate much further. As a modern instance of the vagaries of adaptation, the following German criticism of "The Profligate" in its Teutonic dress may be found amusing, in connection with the English text of the play :—

"The German author may be indebted to the English original of 'Falsche Heilige' for the plan of the piece, and the material for the several acts, but in the entire modelling, in its general character, and in all its merits, it is the play of Blumenthal. It is insinuating and amusing, persuading by fluent, elegant, refined diction, and especially by the sparkling firework witticisms of Blumenthal, which rise like rockets in every scene, while the dramatic *aplomb* is preserved throughout the grand scene in the third act, which did not fail to impress, as the author intended. Blumenthal has shifted the action of the story into the salons of aristocratic Parisian society, and the strongly perfumed atmosphere of the *bons-vivants* and the *grisettes* of Paris, where comfort-loving fathers and guardians compare their marriage-hunting daughters or wards to 'freckles,' which (as the German Hugh Murray says) 'scarcely got rid of, make their reappearance.' The ornaments of the Boulevards are the main characters of the play, but the author (Blumenthal) nowhere disgusts a sensitive listener. He tones down the conversation of the circle, and accentuates its fascinating features, utilising it as a frame for setting his brilliant coruscating jokes. He places contrastingly by the side of the frivolous Don Juan the sentimentally virtuous Paul Benoit, and by the side of the cunning and false Magdalen the innocent child Jeanne de Lunac. The piece is full of rich veins of light and cheerful amusement."

The Australian career of "The Profligate" has been both experimental and successful. Mr. Charles Cartwright and Miss Olga Nethersole produced the play at the Bijou Theatre in Melbourne on Tuesday, June 9, of the present year, and for the first time it was acted in the original version, as now printed. The play ended with Dunstan Renshaw's suicide, a *dénouement* which the Melbourne critics accepted as "more powerfully dramatic" than the reconciliation, but the impression produced upon the public was considered too painful, and on the following Thursday evening the ending of the Garrick version was substituted for the original, and "gave greater satisfaction to the public." Consequently, this is how the play was presented on Tuesday, August 4, 1891, at the Garrick Theatre in Sydney, where it achieved very considerable success, and aroused critical enthusiasm, while it was even then urged that the substitution of the "happy ending," though managerially politic, was calculated to " detract from the actual merits of the play."

MALCOLM C. SALAMAN.

LONDON, *November* 1891.

THE PERSONS OF THE PLAY

WILFRID BRUDENELL

LESLIE, *his sister*

DUNSTAN RENSHAW

JANET PREECE

MR. CHEAL

HUGH MURRAY

MR. EPHGRAVES

LORD DANGARS

MRS. STONEHAY

IRENE, *her daughter*

WEAVER

PRISCILLA

THE PROFLIGATE

THE FIRST ACT

THIS MAN AND THIS WOMAN.

The scene is the junior partner's room in the offices of
MESSRS. CHEAL *and* MURRAY, *solicitors, Furnival's
Inn, Holborn. There is a gloomy air about the
place, with its heavy, old-fashioned furniture, its
oak-panelled walls and dirty white mantelpiece,
and its accumulation of black tin deed-boxes.*

HUGH MURRAY, *a pale, thoughtful, resolute-looking man
of about thirty, plainly dressed, is writing in-
tently at a pedestal-table. He pays no heed to a
knock at the door, which is followed by the entrance of* MR. EPHGRAVES, *an elderly, sober-looking
clerk, who places a slip of paper before him.*

HUGH MURRAY.

Lord Dangars.

EPHGRAVES.

Yes.

HUGH MURRAY.

Mr. Cheal always sees Lord Dangars.

A

EPHGRAVES.

Yes, sir, but Mr. Cheal is so put about by this morning's very unusual business that he doesn't wish to see anybody till after the wedding.

HUGH MURRAY.

Very well.

EPHGRAVES.

[*Handing a bundle of legal documents to* HUGH.] "Dangars v. Dangars." Oh, excuse me, but Mr. Renshaw has sent in some little nosegays with a request that they should be worn to-day. [*Sniffing the flower in his buttonhole.*] As the wedding takes place *from* the office, as it were, I considered it would be a permissible compliment to our client, the bride——

HUGH MURRAY.

Quite so—very kind of Mr. Renshaw.

EPHGRAVES.

I shouldn't have mentioned it, but I see you're not wearing yours.

HUGH MURRAY.

Oh, this is from Mr. Renshaw?

EPHGRAVES.

Yes.

HUGH MURRAY.

We are keeping Lord Dangars waiting.
[EPHGRAVES *goes into the clerk's office, as* HUGH *takes a flower from a glass on the table.*]

I can't wear it—I can't wear it, at *her* wedding.
[EPHGRAVES *ushers in* LORD DANGARS, *a dissipated-
looking man of about forty, dressed in the height
of fashion.*]

LORD DANGARS.

Good morning, Mr. Murray.

HUGH MURRAY.

Good morning. Pray sit down.

LORD DANGARS.

I don't want to bother you, you know, but my
servant, who has been reading the newspapers for
me since my damned—I beg your pardon—since my
divorce business has been before the public, says
that we were in Court again yesterday.

HUGH MURRAY.

Oh, yes. The Decree *Nisi* has been made absolute on the application of the petitioner.

LORD DANGARS.

The Petitioner. Let me see—they call me the
Respondent, don't they ?

HUGH MURRAY.

They do—[*under his breath*] amongst other things.

LORD DANGARS.

It's a deuced odd circumstance that I have been
nearly everything in divorce cases, but *never* a petitioner. Decree *Nisi* made absolute, eh ? That
means I am quite free, doesn't it ?

HUGH MURRAY.

Certainly.

LORD DANGARS.

And eligible ?

HUGH MURRAY.

I beg pardon ?

LORD DANGARS.

I can marry again ?

HUGH MURRAY.

You could marry again if you thought proper.

LORD DANGARS.

You wouldn't call it improper ?

HUGH MURRAY.

If you ask me that as your solicitor I answer No. Otherwise I have what are perhaps peculiar notions as to the eligibility of a man who marries.

LORD DANGARS.

Oh, have you ! Well, I don't see that a man's eligibility requires any further qualification than that of his being single. You differ ?

HUGH MURRAY.

May I speak honestly, Lord Dangars ?

LORD DANGARS.

Do. I admire anything of that sort. I think your partner told me you were a Scotchman and new to London. I like to encounter a man in his honest stage.

HUGH MURRAY.

Thank you. Then you will allow me to maintain that the man who marries a good woman knowing that his past life is not as spotless as hers grievously wrongs his wife and fools himself.

LORD DANGARS.

As for wronging *her*, that's an abstract question of sentiment. But I don't see how the man is a fool.

HUGH MURRAY.

A man is a fool to bind himself to one who soon-er or later must learn what little need there is to respect her husband.

LORD DANGARS.

Why, my dear Mr. Murray, you're actually put-ting men on a level with ladies. Ladies, I admit, are like nations—to be happy they should have no histories. But don't you know that Marriage is the tomb of the Past, as far as a man is concerned?

HUGH MURRAY.

No, I don't know it and I don't believe it.

LORD DANGARS.

Oh, really——

HUGH MURRAY.

You can't lay the Past: it has an ugly habit of breaking its tomb.

LORD DANGARS.

Even then the shades of pretty women should not be such very bad company. [*Referring to his watch.*] By Jove, a pleasant chat runs into one's time. If you want me, " *Poste Restante*, Rome," till you hear again.

HUGH MURRAY.

Going abroad, during the shooting?

LORD DANGARS.

I must, you know. This divorce business checks the pleasant flow of invitations for a season or two. So I shall spend a few months tranquilly in Italy and write a Society novel.

HUGH MURRAY.

A Society novel!

LORD DANGARS.

Yes—that seems the only thing left for a man whose reputation is a little off colour. Good-bye, Mr. Murray.

HUGH MURRAY.

Good-bye, Lord Dangars. Come this way.
[HUGH *opens the door leading on to the staircase-landing.*]

LORD DANGARS.

Excuse me, but didn't I see Mr. Dunstan Renshaw enter your outer office just then?

HUGH MURRAY.

I am expecting Mr. Renshaw. Do you know him?

LORD DANGARS.

Know him! We're bosom friends.

HUGH MURRAY.

Friends? You and Mr. Renshaw? Then of course you know that he is going to be married this morning.

LORD DANGARS.

Married! You're joking!

HUGH MURRAY.

I have a perfectly serious engagement to accompany Mr. Renshaw to the Registrar's in half-an-hour.

LORD DANGARS.

You! No! Ha, ha! That's very good—that's very good—that's capital!

HUGH MURRAY.

Why does the idea of Mr. Renshaw's marriage amuse you so much, Lord Dangars?

LORD DANGARS.

My dear Mr. Murray, I am not laughing at Renshaw's marriage, but it tickles me confoundedly to think that you, my Quixotic young friend, are to assist at laying the marble slab upon dear old Dunstan's bachelor days—and nights.

HUGH MURRAY.

You mean that Mr. Renshaw is not, according to my qualification, an eligible husband for a pure honest-hearted woman?

LORD DANGARS.

Oh, come, come, Mr. Murray, let us be men of the world. Renshaw's a good fellow, just one of my own sort; that's all I mean. [HUGH *turns away impatiently.*] May I beg to know who's the lady?

HUGH MURRAY.

Miss Leslie Brudenell—an orphan—my partner's ward.

LORD DANGARS.

Money? I needn't ask.

HUGH MURRAY.

If Miss Brudenell were penniless I should describe her as a millionaire. She is very sweet, very beautiful.

LORD DANGARS.

You're enthusiastic.

HUGH MURRAY.

No, barely just. [*Speaking half to himself.*] I thought the same the moment I first saw her. She was walking in the grounds of the old school-house at Helmstead, and I stood aside in the shade of the beeches and watched her—I couldn't help it. And I remember how I stammered when I spoke to her; because some women are like sacred pictures, you can't do more than whisper before them. That's only six month's ago, and to-day—— God forgive us if we are doing wrong!

LORD DANGARS.

[*To himself.*] I'm dashed if my pious young Scotch solicitor isn't in love with the girl himself.

[EPHGRAVES *comes from the clerk's office.*]

HUGH MURRAY.

Mr. Renshaw?

EPHGRAVES.

Yes.

LORD DANGARS.

Dunstan!

DUNSTAN RENSHAW.

[*Speaking outside.*] Why, George!

[DUNSTAN RENSHAW *enters as* EPHGRAVES *retires. He is a handsome young man with a buoyant self-possessed manner, looking not more than thirty, but with the signs of a dissolute life in his face; his clothes are fashionable and suggest the bridegroom.*]

DUNSTAN RENSHAW.

Congratulate you! So the law has turned you into a jolly old bachelor?

LORD DANGARS.

Yes, my boy—on condition that my solicitor offers a young fresh victim to Hymen in the course of this morning.

DUNSTAN RENSHAW.

Hallo! You know all about it, do you?

LORD DANGARS.

Mr. Murray broke the news as gently as possible.

DUNSTAN RENSHAW.

[*Shaking hands with* MURRAY.] My best man. Good morning, Murray. Was it a shock, George?

LORD DANGARS.

Terrible! You might have knocked me down with one of Clotilda Green's lace fans.

Dunstan Renshaw.

Shut up, now! I've played that sort of game out; so no reminiscences.

Lord Dangars.

Trust me, my dear boy. Make me a friend of your hearth and edit my recollections.

Dunstan Renshaw.

Then all you remember is that at Cambridge I was a diligent but unlucky student.

Lord Dangars.

Quite so—I recollect that perfectly.

Dunstan Renshaw.

And that from boyhood I have suffered from a stupefying bashfulness before women.

Lord Dangars.

Done. You'll recall the same of me when I next have occasion to marry, won't you?

Dunstan Renshaw.

It's a bargain. I— [*Puts his hand over his eyes.*] Oh, confound this!

Lord Dangars.

What's the matter? Are you ill?

Dunstan Renshaw.

No. Wait a minute. There were some fellows at my lodgings last night assisting at the launching of the ship—I mean, saying good-bye to me. [*Supports himself unsteadily with the back of a chair.*] They set light to a bowlful of brandy and threw my latchkey into it—awful fun. And then they all swore they'd see the last of me, and they stayed and stayed till they couldn't see anything at all.

[*He sinks on to the chair, with his head resting on his hands.* HUGH *brings him a glass of water.*]

HUGH MURRAY.

Here.

DUNSTAN RENSHAW.

Thanks. [*Gradually recovering.*] I'm all right. Did I look white or yellow?

LORD DANGARS.

Neither — green. Fortunate the lady was not present.

DUNSTAN RENSHAW.

Oh, Miss Brudenell doesn't know why rooms sometimes go round and round.

LORD DANGARS.

No? Perhaps her relations are more penetrating.

DUNSTAN RENSHAW.

Thank goodness there are no such incumbrances. Leslie is an orphan; I'm an orphan. I'm alone in the world; she has only a young brother who doesn't count. So we start at even weights.

[*He drains the remainder of the water and shivers.*]

LORD DANGARS.

Met her at a ball, of course. I really will be seen at dances again by-and-by.

DUNSTAN RENSHAW.

A ball—nonsense. Her only idea of a ball is a lot

of girls sitting against a wall pulling crackers. She's
a "little maid from school."

LORD DANGARS.

Charming! But how——

DUNSTAN RENSHAW.

How—I'll give you the recipe. Go down into the
country for a couple of days' fishing.

LORD DANGARS.

Often done it—caught fish, no girls.

DUNSTAN RENSHAW.

Wait. The stream must run off your host's prop-
erty through the recreation grounds of a young ladies' school.

LORD DANGARS.

Times are altered—there was always a brick wall
in my day.

DUNSTAN RENSHAW.

Brick walls still exist, but a heavy fish on your
line breaks down your notions of propriety and you
paddle along mid-stream. You soon discover some
pretty little women with their arms round each
other's waists, and you apologise profusely.

LORD DANGARS.

But you risk rheumatism.

DUNSTAN RENSHAW.

So Leslie thought, and that won me her sympathy.

LORD DANGARS.

And sympathy is akin to love.

DUNSTAN RENSHAW.

And love, occasionally, leads to marriage. [*Holding out his hand to* DANGARS, *who buttons his glove.*] Help deck me for the sacrifice, George. As luck would have it, Leslie's guardian, Mr. Cheal, was my people's lawyer years ago, and he knew I was a gentleman and all that sort of thing. So Cheal got my affairs into something like order, made me settle everything on Leslie, and now you behold in me a happy bridegroom with a headache fit to convert the devil. Thanks, old man.

[MR. CHEAL *comes from his private office. He is an elderly man with a pompous manner and florid complexion.*]

MR. CHEAL.

Hasn't Miss Brudenell arrived yet? Ah, good morning, Lord Dangars. Mr. Renshaw, pray don't be late. I believe it is customary for the bridegroom to receive the lady at the Registrar's. Who is a married man here? Oh, Lord Dangars, perhaps *you* can tell us.

DUNSTAN RENSHAW.

No, no! Ask him something about the Divorce Court.

MR. CHEAL.

Good gracious, I quite forgot! Pray pardon me.
[DUNSTAN *laughs heartily.*]

DUNSTAN RENSHAW.

I'm waiting for Mr. Murray, my best man.

MR. CHEAL.

[*Rather testily.*] Mr. Murray! [HUGH *is gazing into the fire.*] Mr. Murray, please.

HUGH MURRAY.

Eh?

MR. CHEAL.

Mr. Renshaw is waiting.

HUGH MURRAY.

I beg your pardon, Mr. Renshaw. I must ask you to dispense with my assistance this morning.

[*He sits at his table and commences writing, while* CHEAL, DUNSTAN, *and* DANGARS *exchange glances.*]

DUNSTAN RENSHAW.

Oh, all right—don't mention it.

LORD DANGARS.

[*To himself.*] Thought so.

MR. CHEAL.

You place us in rather an awkward position, Mr. Murray. I have to escort Miss Brudenell, and I hardly wish to send a clerk with Mr. Renshaw.

DUNSTAN RENSHAW.

Look here, don't bother. Where does this Registrar chap hang out?

MR. CHEAL.

Twenty-three, Ely Place—very near here.

LORD DANGARS.

I'll walk with you, my boy, and lend you my moral support.

DUNSTAN RENSHAW.

Thanks. But, excuse me, George, I think we'll part company at the Registrar's front door.

LORD DANGARS.

You believe in omens then, eh?

DUNSTAN RENSHAW.

Well, every man does on his wedding morning.

LORD DANGARS.

All right. Do you think I want to assist at your wedding? You never came to hear my divorce case.

[DANGARS *leaves the office followed by* DUNSTAN.]

MR. CHEAL.

Really, Mr. Murray, this is scarcely business-like.

HUGH MURRAY.

I think it is all cruelly business-like. Mr. Cheal, don't you think it possible, even at this moment, to stop this marriage?

MR. CHEAL.

Stop the marriage! Good gracious, sir, for what reason?

HUGH MURRAY.

The marriage of a simple-minded trustful school-girl to a man of whom you know either too little or too much.

MR. CHEAL.

I know a great deal of Mr. Renshaw. He comes of a very excellent family—excellent family.

HUGH MURRAY.

Are the members of it at hand to speak for him?

MR. CHEAL.

They are all, I hope, beyond the reach of preju-dice, Mr. Murray. They are unhappily deceased.

HUGH MURRAY.

Then how can you weigh the dead against the living? Here are two lives to be brought together this morning or kept apart, as *you* will; for upon you rests the responsibility of this marriage.

MR. CHEAL.

I beg your pardon, Mr. Murray. I should have thought that a young gentleman of your severe training would scarcely need to be reminded that marriages are——

HUGH MURRAY.

Made in Heaven?

MR. CHEAL.

Yes, sir, certainly.

HUGH MURRAY.

This one, sir, is the exclusive manufacture of Hol-born.

MR. CHEAL.

That's rather a flippant observation, Mr. Murray.

HUGH MURRAY.

I doubt whether Providence is ever especially busy in promoting the union of a delicate-minded child with a coarse gross-natured profligate.

MR. CHEAL.

Mr. Murray, you are speaking of a client in terms to which I prefer being no party. Mr. Renshaw may have yielded to some of the lighter temptations not unknown even in my youth—except to those employed in legal studies. But the world is not apt to condemn the—the——

HUGH MURRAY.

The license it permits itself!

MR. CHEAL.

You are bullying the world, Mr. Murray. I don't attempt, sir, to be much wiser than the world.

HUGH MURRAY.

But it costs so small an effort to be a little better. I tell you I have stood by and heard this man Renshaw laughing over his excesses with the airs of a vicious school-boy.

MR. CHEAL.

Tut, tut, that's all past. Marriage is the real beginning of a man's life.

HUGH MURRAY.

No, sir, it is the end of it—what comes after is either heaven or hell.

[EPHGRAVES *enters.*]

EPHGRAVES.

Miss Brudenell is here with her maid and Mr. Wilfrid.

HUGH MURRAY.

Don't bring them in till I ring.

D

MR. CHEAL.

Really, Mr. Murray—— !   [EPHGRAVES *retires.*]

HUGH MURRAY.

Mr. Cheal, I make a final appeal to you with my whole heart.

MR. CHEAL.

I am a man of business, Mr. Murray !

HUGH MURRAY.

I know that; and I know that this child is an unremunerative responsibility of which you would gladly be rid.

MR. CHEAL.

Frankly, the trustees were most inadequately provided for under the Will.

HUGH MURRAY.

Very well—relieve yourself of the trust and throw the estate into Chancery, and from this moment I undertake to bear on my shoulders the responsibilities of Miss Brudenell's future.

MR. CHEAL.

My dear sir, you talk as if the young lady were not deeply in love with Mr. Renshaw.

HUGH MURRAY.

What judge is a school-girl of the worth of a man ?   Of course she falls in love with the first she meets.

MR. CHEAL.

Nothing of the kind.   Why, for that matter, Miss Brudenell knew *you* before she met Mr. Renshaw.

HUGH MURRAY.

Yes, yes—I know!

MR. CHEAL.

You have been down to the school at Helmstead often enough—why on earth didn't the child fall in love with you?

HUGH MURRAY.

No—true, true. But I have no pretensions to—— of course—I—— [*He strikes a bell.*] I fear my argument has been very poor.

[EPHGRAVES *ushers in* LESLIE BRUDENELL, *a sweet-looking girl, tastefully but simply dressed, who is accompanied by her brother* WILFRID, *a handsome, boyish young man of about one-and-twenty, and her maid* PRISCILLA, *a healthy-looking country girl.*]

LESLIE.

Oh, Mr. Cheal, am I late?

MR. CHEAL.

Late, my dear—no. Good morning, Mr. Brudenell.

WILFRID BRUDENELL.

Leslie was ready to start at seven o'clock this morning and broke the hotel-bell ringing for breakfast.

LESLIE.

Oh, don't tell about me, Will, dear.

MR. CHEAL.

Let me know when the carriage arrives, Mr. Ephgraves.

EPHGRAVES.

Yes, sir.   [EPHGRAVES *goes out.*]

LESLIE.

[*Offering her hand.*] Mr. Murray.

HUGH MURRAY.

Were you very frightened lest you should be late ?

LESLIE.

Yes, *very*.

HUGH MURRAY.

Of course you were.

LESLIE.

For *his* sake—he would suffer so if I kept him waiting. Where is he ?

HUGH MURRAY.

At the Registrar's.

LESLIE.

Why aren't you with him ? You promised.

HUGH MURRAY.

I am busy.

LESLIE.

Oh, how unkind to be busy on such a morning ! Will, Mr. Murray won't come to the wedding.

WILFRID BRUDENELL.

That's a shame. How d'y'r do, Mr. Murray ?

MR. CHEAL.

H'm ! *I* shall be there.

WILFRID BRUDENELL.

Yes, but Leslie wants her London Mother as well as her London Father.

MR. CHEAL.

Eh? What's that?

LESLIE.

Nothing—be quiet, Will!

MR. CHEAL.

What is the meaning of a London father and——

WILFRID BRUDENELL.

I'll tell you——

LESLIE.

No, no—you tell things so roughly. My London Father is a name the school-girls gave you, Mr. Cheal, because you are my guardian in London and look after me. And when Mr. Murray began to come down to Helmstead about once a month to see that I was happy, they set about to invent some title for him too. And as I couldn't have two fathers and I already had a real brother they called Mr. Murray my London Mother, because he was so thoughtful and tender, just as my school-fellows told me their mothers are.

MR. CHEAL.

H'm! Well, my dear, all that is very nice for school-girls, but it is what practical people call stuff and nonsense. I'll go and get my hat.

[*He goes out.*]

LESLIE.

Mr. Cheal is angry.

Hugh Murray.

No, no.

Leslie.

He is. He said "stuff and nonsense" the other day when I begged him to let me be married in a church, and now——

Hugh Murray.

Ah, don't think of Mr. Cheal's very business-like manner.

Leslie.

I can't help it. Tell me, Mr. Murray, does everything simple become stuff and nonsense when you get married?

Hugh Murray.

How should I know, my child? I am an old bachelor. [Priscilla *beckons* Leslie.]

Priscilla.

Missy—Miss—you're untidy again!

Leslie.

Oh, no, don't say that!
[Priscilla *arranges* Leslie's *costume.*]

Leslie.

The little mirror, Priscilla. [*Surveying herself critically as the sunlight enters at the windows.*] Priscilla, I'm getting uglier as the day wears on.

Priscilla.

I'm sure you're quite good-looking enough for London, Miss.

LESLIE.

I'm not thinking about London.

WILFRID BRUDENELL.

[*Addressing* HUGH.] That's an odd picture for a lawyer's musty office.

HUGH MURRAY.

Ay—imagine what would become of a plain matter-of-fact lawyer, sitting here scribbling day after day, if he could never get that vision out of his eyes.

WILFRID BRUDENELL.

Rather bad for his clients, eh ?

HUGH MURRAY.

Yes, and bad for the lawyer.

LESLIE.

I hope the Registrar's office is very dark, Mr. Murray. I particularly dislike my face to-day.

PRISCILLA.

[*Whispering to* HUGH.] Ain't she sweet and pretty, sir ?

HUGH MURRAY.

Yes.

PRISCILLA.

A lucky gentleman Mr. Renshaw, sir.

HUGH MURRAY.

Ay.

LESLIE.

I heard that. Indeed Mr. Renshaw is not lucky at all

HUGH MURRAY

I think so. Why not?

LESLIE.

Because I am not worthy of him. You're his friend, Mr. Murray, and you know how generous and true he is. I can tell you, my London Mother, that every night and morning since I have been engaged, I have prayed nothing but this, over and over again—" Make me good enough—good enough for Dunstan Renshaw!" [HUGH *moves away.*] [*Looking at herself in the mirror.*] I wish now I had added " make me a little prettier."

[EPHGRAVES *appears at the door.*]

EPHGRAVES.

The carriage is here, sir.

LESLIE and PRISCILLA.

Oh!

HUGH MURRAY.

Tell Mr. Cheal.
[LESLIE *is a little flurried, and* PRISCILLA *at once busies herself about* LESLIE'S *costume.*]

EPHGRAVES.

A young lady is in my room waiting to see you, Mr. Murray. She brings a card of Mr. Wilfrid's with your name on it in his writing.

WILFRID BRUDENELL.

Oh, I am so glad she has called! Mr. Murray, I've found your firm a new client.

HUGH MURRAY.

Indeed—thank you—thank you. In a few mo-
ments, Mr. Ephgraves.

[EPHGRAVES *goes into the inner office.*]

WILFRID BRUDENELL.

It's quite a romance, isn't it, Leslie?

LESLIE.

Oh, don't speak to me, please, dear.

WILFRID BRUDENELL.

When Leslie and I arrived at Paddington Station
last night, a solitary young lady got out of the next
compartment. Les, wasn't she gentle and pretty?

LESLIE.

Yes—yes. There's a button off my glove.

[PRISCILLA *hastily produces needle and thread and
commences stitching the glove.*]

WILFRID BRUDENELL.

The poor little thing seemed quite lost in the
crowd and bustle and at last, pushed about by the
porters and passengers, she sat herself down to cry.
We asked if we could help her. Do you remember
how pretty she looked then, Les?

LESLIE.

I can't remember anything till I have been married a little while. Do be quick, Priscilla.

WILFRID BRUDENELL.

Well, what do you think the poor little lady
wanted? She wanted to find the cleverest man in

London, some one to advise her on an awfully important matter. Leslie said *I* was clever, didn't you, Les?

LESLIE.

Yes, but I *thought* of Mr. Renshaw.

WILFRID BRUDENELL.

But, said I, "I know what you really need—a lawyer," and I gave her my card to present to Mr. Hugh Murray, of Cheal and Murray, Furnival's Inn.

HUGH MURRAY.

Thank you—thank you.

WILFRID BRUDENELL.

[*To himself.*] I wish I could find her here when we come back.   [CHEAL *bustles into the room.*]

MR. CHEAL.

Now then, my dear, are you ready?

LESLIE.

Ready! You had better say farewell to Miss Leslie Brudenell, Mr. Murray; you will never see her again.

HUGH MURRAY.

Good-bye.

LESLIE.

Come to my wedding.

HUGH MURRAY.

I—I am busy.

              [*He turns away and sits at his desk.*]

LESLIE.

[*To herself.*] I wonder whether the world will be of the same colour when I am married? Mr. Murray seems changing already.

MR. CHEAL.

My dear!
  [CHEAL *offers his arm to* LESLIE, *who, as she takes it, looks appealingly at* HUGH, *but he will not notice her.*]

LESLIE.

Mr. Murray! Mr. Murray!
  [*She leaves the room on* CHEAL's *arm, attended by* PRISCILLA.]

WILFRID BRUDENELL.

I say, we shan't be long getting married. I wish you could detain the young lady till I return.

HUGH MURRAY.

Yes—yes.

WILFRID BRUDENELL.

It's of no consequence, you know.
  [WILFRID *runs out after the wedding party.*]

HUGH MURRAY.

She is going. [*He goes to the window and looks out.*] Ah! They have taken her away. The Inn is empty.
  [EPHGRAVES *enters.*]

EPHGRAVES.

H'm! Mr. Murray.

HUGH MURRAY.

They have gone, Ephgraves.

EPHGRAVES.

Yes. [*Handing him a slip of paper.*] Will you see the young lady now?

HUGH MURRAY.

Certainly. [EPHGRAVES *goes out.*]

HUGH MURRAY.

[*Reading.*] "Miss Janet Preece, introduced by Mr. Wilfrid Brudenell."

[EPHGRAVES *ushers in* JANET PREECE. *a pretty, simply-dressed girl of about eighteen, with a timid air, and a troubled look.*]

JANET PREECE.

Are you Mr. Murray, sir?

HUGH MURRAY.

Yes. Sit down there. You wish to see a solicitor, I understand?

JANET PREECE.

A lawyer, sir.

HUGH MURRAY.

That's the same thing—sometimes. In what way can I serve you?

JANET PREECE.

I—I thought you would be older.

HUGH MURRAY.

Mr. Cheal, my partner, is older than I, but he is out. Can't you believe in me?

JANET PREECE.

It isn't that I think you're not clever.

HUGH MURRAY.

Come, come, that's something.

JANET PREECE.

But you don't know why I—what I have to—
Heaven help me !

HUGH MURRAY.

You know, people bring their troubles to men
like me quite as an ordinary matter ——

JANET PREECE.

Yes, sir — ordinary troubles. I could tell a
woman : I could tell your wife if she was as kind as
you seem to be.

HUGH MURRAY.

My dear young lady, I have no wife. Come now,
don't think of me as anything but a mere machine.

[*He listens without looking at her.*]

JANET PREECE.

I — want — to — find somebody who has disap-
peared.

HUGH MURRAY.

Yes ? A man or a woman ?

JANET PREECE.

A man.

HUGH MURRAY.

The task may be very easy or very difficult. Is
he a London man ?

JANET PREECE.

Yes, a town gentleman who does ill in the country.

HUGH MURRAY.

Shall I begin by writing down his name?

JANET PREECE.

I don't know his name—I only know the name he
called himself by away down home. Mr.—Lawrence—Kenward. Lawrence—Kenward—Esquire.

HUGH MURRAY.

How do you know the name is assumed?

JANET PREECE.

Because I once came softly into the room while
he was signing a letter; he wrote only his initials,
but I saw that they didn't belong to the name of
Lawrence Kenward.

HUGH MURRAY.

What were the initials?

JANET PREECE.

D. R.

HUGH MURRAY.

[*Scribbling upon a sheet of paper.*] Ah, you may
have been mistaken. The letters "D. R." and "L.
K." have some resemblance at a distance.

JANET PREECE.

No—no, no—no!

HUGH MURRAY.

[*Scribbling again.*] Now, making the "D. R." in
this way—[*thoughtfully*] D. R.

JANET PREECE.

I'm not mistaken, for when I charged him with deceiving me he told me a falsehood with his lips and the truth with his eyes. And that night he broke with me.

HUGH MURRAY.

[*To himself, looking at his watch.*] It is *her* name now. Why do I let everything remind me of it? D. R. [*To* JANET.] Have you any letter from this man?

JANET PREECE.

No. He was always too near me for the need of writing, the more's the shame.

HUGH MURRAY.

Have you his portrait—a photograph?

JANET PREECE.

He always meant me too much ill to give me a portrait.

HUGH MURRAY.

Describe him.

JANET PREECE.

A man about your age, sir, I should guess, but with a boy's voice when he speaks to women. I—I —I can't describe him.

HUGH MURRAY.

[*To himself.*] Great Heavens! If by any awful freak of fate this poor creature is a victim of Renshaw's—and *she* at this moment standing beside him——! What a fool I am to think of no man but Renshaw!

JANET PREECE.

Don't ask me to describe him in words, sir,—I can't, I can't. But I've taught myself to draw his face faithfully. I'm not boasting—I can't draw anything else because I see nothing else. Give me some paper I can sketch upon, and a pencil.

[HUGH *hands her paper and pencil, and watches while she sketches.*]

HUGH MURRAY.

[*To himself.*] If the face she sketches should bear any resemblance to his, what could I do, what could I do?

JANET PREECE.

[*To herself.*] That's with his mocking look as I last saw him. He is always mocking me now.

HUGH MURRAY.

[*To himself.*] I could do nothing—it's too late—nothing. Shall I look now? No. What a coward I am! Yes. [*He looks over* JANET'S *shoulder.*] Renshaw! [*He struggles against his agitation.*] The wife! I must think of the wife. [*To* JANET.] My poor child, the most accurate portrait in the world is poor material towards hunting for a man in this labyrinth of London.

JANET PREECE.

Oh, but take it. His face must be familiar to hundreds of men and women in London. I know that he belongs to some of your great clubs and goes to the race-meetings in grand style—he has

told me so. And take these. These papers tell
you all about me and give an address where you
can write to me when you've traced him.

HUGH MURRAY.

I—I can't undertake this search. It's useless—
it's useless.

JANET PREECE.

No, no—don't refuse to help me! Your face says
you are clever—it's easy work for you. He isn't in
hiding; he is flaunting about in broad sunlight in
your fine parks, maybe with another poor simple
girl on his arm. Find him for me! He isn't a
murderer stealing along in the shadow of walls at
night-time — he is only a betrayer of women, and
men don't hide for that!

HUGH MURRAY.

I—I'll look through this bundle of papers. You
shall hear from me to-morrow.

[*He is showing* JANET *to the door when* WILFRID
enters.]

WILFRID BRUDENELL.

Oh, I'm so glad you've found your way here!
How strange that we should meet again!

JANET PREECE.

Yes. Thank you, thank you for your kindness.
Good-bye! [*She goes hurriedly from the room.*]

WILFRID BRUDENELL.

There now! After my hurrying off on the chance
of seeing her, and being nearly run down in Holborn—only "thank you" and "good-bye!"

HUGH MURRAY.

Have they left the Registrar's?

WILFRID BRUDENELL.

He was congratulating them when I stole away.

HUGH MURRAY.

[*To himself.*] If the poor girl should come face to face with Renshaw this morning!
[HUGH *looks out of the window.*]

WILFRID BRUDENELL.

Come now, Mr. Murray, isn't she sweet?

HUGH MURRAY.

Yes, yes. [*Then to himself.*] She is crossing the Inn.

WILFRID BRUDENELL.

And don't you thank me for sending you such a pretty client?

HUGH MURRAY.

[*Turning away from the window.*] She's gone.

WILFRID BRUDENELL.

Do tell me about her. What's her name? I should like to think of her by some name.

HUGH MURRAY.

A lawyer talks of everything but his clients, my boy. So—your sister is married, eh?

WILFRID BRUDENELL.

Married! She was married before one's eyes became used to the darkness of the gloomy little office.

HUGH MURRAY.

Married—fast married!.

WILFRID BRUDENELL.

The older I grow the more positive I am that
nothing in life takes any time to speak of. You're
born in no time, you're married in no time, you live
no time, you die in no time, you're forgotten in no
time——

HUGH MURRAY.

But you suffer all the time.

WILFRID BRUDENELL.

Suffer! Leslie and I intend never to suffer. We
sat up together late last night, hand in hand, and
we entered into a compact that we'll remain to each
other simple, light-hearted boy and girl for ever and
ever. That's the way to be happy. Hark! [*He
opens the door.*] Here they are! Hallo, Dunstan!

[RENSHAW *enters, followed by his man,* WEAVER, *who
carries his travelling coat and hat.*]

DUNSTAN RENSHAW.

It's all over, Mr. Murray. Ha, ha! Leslie was on
the verge of tears because the Registrar wouldn't
read the Marriage Service. What do you want,
Weaver?

WEAVER.

If you mean to get to Cannon Street, to catch the
12.37 for Folkestone, you haven't any time to lose,
sir.

DUNSTAN RENSHAW.

Oh. [*To* WILFRID.] Leslie is affixing her signature,
with a great deal of dignity, to some legal documents in the next room.   Ask her to omit the flour-
ishes, Wilfrid ; there's a good fellow.

[WILFRID *goes quickly into the clerk's office followed by* WEAVER.]

DUNSTAN RENSHAW.

[*Hums an air and yawns.*] I say, Murray, if you
ever marry, take my advice—patronize the Registrar ; the process is rapid and merciful.

HUGH MURRAY.

Mr. Renshaw, I don't stand in need of your coun-
sel on the question of marriage, but less than half
an hour ago you might with profit to yourself have
asked for mine.

DUNSTAN RENSHAW.

What's the matter ?   What's wrong ?

HUGH MURRAY.

I tell you to your face, you have done a cruel, a
wanton act !

DUNSTAN RENSHAW.

What do you mean ?

HUGH MURRAY.

I know your past !   I know that your mind is
vicious and your heart callous ; and yet you have
dared to join lives with a child whose knowledge of
evil is a blank and whose instincts are pure and
beautiful—God forgive you !

DUNSTAN RENSHAW.

Mr. Murray, the tone you're good enough to adopt deserves some special recognition. But you've always, I understand, been very kind to Leslie, and I don't choose to dispute with one of her friends on her wedding morning.

HUGH MURRAY.

You can't dispute with me because there is no question of truth between us !

DUNSTAN RENSHAW.

Oh, as to my past, which you are pleased to wax mightily moral about, well—I have taken the world as I found it——

HUGH MURRAY.

You chant the litany of these who rifle and wrong ! You have simply taken the world's evil as you found it ! I warn you !

DUNSTAN RENSHAW.

And I warn *you* that you'll do badly as a lawyer. Try the pulpit.

HUGH MURRAY.

I warn you ! As surely as we now stand face to face, the crime you commit to-day you will expiate bitterly !

DUNSTAN RENSHAW.

Thank you for your warning, Mr. Murray. It is my intention to expiate my atrocities by a life of tolerable ease and comfort. [*Looking at his watch.*] We shall really lose our train.

HUGH MURRAY.

[*Turning away in disgust.*]   Oh!

DUNSTAN RENSHAW.

And it may surprise a sentimental Scotch gentleman like yourself to learn that marriages of contentment are the reward of husbands who have
taken the precaution to sow their wild oats rather
thickly.

HUGH MURRAY.

Contentment!

DUNSTAN RENSHAW.

Yes—I've studied the question.

HUGH MURRAY.

Contentment! Renshaw, do you imagine there
is no Autumn in the life of a profligate? Do you
think there is no moment when the accursed crop
begins to rear its millions of heads above ground;
when the rich man would give his wealth to be able
to tread them back into the earth which rejects the
foul load? To-day, you have robbed some honest
man of a sweet companion!

DUNSTAN RENSHAW.

Look here, Mr. Murray—— !

HUGH MURRAY.

To-morrow, next week, next month, you may be
happy—but what of the time when those wild oats
thrust their ears through the very seams of the floor
trodden by the wife whose respect you will have
learned to covet! You may drag her into the
crowded streets—there is the same vile growth

springing up from the chinks of the pavement! In your house or in the open, the scent of the mildewed grain always in your nostrils, and in your ears no music but the wind's rustle amongst the fat sheaves! And, worst of all, your wife's heart a granary bursting with the load of shame your profligacy has stored there! I warn you—Mr. Lawrence Kenward!

DUNSTAN RENSHAW.

What! Hold your tongue, man; d——n you, hold your tongue!

[LESLIE *enters with* WILFRID *and* CHEAL.]

LESLIE.

[*To* DUNSTAN.] Have I kept you waiting? You're not cross with me, Dun, dear?

DUNSTAN RENSHAW.

Cross—no. But— [*looking sullenly at* HUGH] let us get on our journey.

LESLIE.

Good-bye, Mr. Murray. [*He takes her hand.*] Won't you—won't you congratulate Mrs. Dunstan Renshaw? Do say something to me!

HUGH MURRAY.

What can I say to you but this—God bless you, little school-girl, always?

[*She joins* DUNSTAN *and goes out, followed by* WILFRID *and* CHEAL. HUGH *is left alone gazing after them.*]

END OF THE FIRST ACT.

THE SECOND ACT.

THE SWORD OF DAMOCLES.

The scene is the Loggia of the Villa Colobiano, a beautiful old Florentine villa on the road to Fiesole, with a view of Florence in the distance. It is an artistic-looking place, with elegant pillars supporting a painted ceiling, coloured marble flooring, and a handsome balustrade and steps leading to the road and garden below, while noticeable on the wall of the villa, between the two entrance windows, is a glass case protecting the remnants of an old, half-obliterated fresco.

WEAVER is gazing down the road through a pair of field-glasses, and PRISCILLA is bringing in the tea things, which she proceeds to arrange on a little table.

WEAVER.

Pris.

PRISCILLA.

Hush! [*Pointing towards the inner room.*] Mr. Wilfrid has gone right off, tired out with his travelling.

WEAVER.

I'm very sorry, but what am I to do? Here's a carriage, with some ladies, coming up the road;

of course they'll pull up here to look at our blessed cartoon.

PRISCILLA.

Well, whatever folks can see in them few smears and scratches to come botherin' us about, passes my belief.

WEAVER.

You don't see nothing in it, of course—a country-bred girl. But there's a real bit of Michael Angelo under that glass. When he was stayin' in this 'ouse some time back he amused himself by drawing that with a piece of black chalk.

PRISCILLA.

Why don't he send and fetch it away?

WEAVER.

It's on the wall of the villa—how can he fetch it? And then again, he's dead. [*A bell rings.*] I said so.

PRISCILLA.

Bother it! It's sp'iled my dear little missy's honeymoon. Jest as master is stroking the back of her little 'and, or dear missy is a' goin' to droop her head on master's shoulder, in comes Weaver with "Somebody to look at the wall!" Lovin' master as she do, why don't she wipe it off and a' done with it!

[MRS. STONEHAY'S *voice is heard within the house.*]

MRS. STONEHAY.

There is a step there, Irene—I have already struck my foot.

PRISCILLA.

Hush ! Don't show it 'em, Weaver.

WEAVER.

I must. The villa was let to us on condition that all visitors was allowed to see the cartoon. This way, please.

[*He shows in* MRS. STONEHAY, *a pompous-looking woman with an arrogant and artificial manner, and her daughter* IRENE, *a handsome girl of about twenty, cold in speech and bearing.*]

MRS. STONEHAY.

I hope we have not toiled up two flights of stairs for nothing. What is there to be seen here ?

PRISCILLA.

[*Pointing to* WILFRID.] Please, ma'am, the young gentleman has just travelled right through from England, and has fallen asleep.

MRS. STONEHAY.

Oh, indeed. This is surely not *all*.

WEAVER.

[*Opening the glass case.*] Here is the cartoon, ma'am.

MRS. STONEHAY.

Cartoon—where ?

WEAVER.

A allegorical design, by Michael Angelo, ma'am ; done when he was stayin' in this very 'ouse.

MRS. STONEHAY.

Quite interesting ! [*Pedantically*] Michael Angelo.

WEAVER.

Michael Angelo.

MRS. STONEHAY.

How superior to the cartoons in our English comic journals! Irene.

IRENE.

Yes, mamma?

MRS. STONEHAY.

Come here, child. [*To* WEAVER.] What is the subject?

WEAVER.

The Break of Day, ma'am. The black cloud underneath is departin' Night—the nood figure reclinin' on it is Early Morning.

MRS. STONEHAY.

Ugh! Never mind, Irene.

IRENE.

Mamma, do you remember a girl who was at school at Helmstead during my last term—a little thing named Brudenell?

MRS. STONEHAY.

No—why?

IRENE.

I am certain that the boy asleep there is the brother who came down every Saturday to visit her.

MRS. STONEHAY.

Dear me! [*To* PRISCILLA.] My good girl. Is that young gentleman's name Brudenell?

PRISCILLA.

Yes, ma'am. It's Mr. Wilfrid, Mrs. Renshaw's brother.

MRS. STONEHAY.

Mrs. Renshaw! Miss Brudenell is married?

PRISCILLA.

A month ago, ma'am.

MRS. STONEHAY.

At home, I hope?

PRISCILLA.

She's with Mr. Renshaw in the garden, ma'am.

MRS. STONEHAY.

[*Giving* PRISCILLA *a card.*] Your mistress will be delighted to see Mrs. Stonehay and her daughter. She is well and happy?

PRISCILLA.

As happy as the day is long, ma'am.

[PRISCILLA *disappears down the steps.*]

MRS. STONEHAY.

Irene, this will save us the expense of tea at Fiesole. [*To* WEAVER.] Oh, you will find a young lady outside—my companion; be good enough to tell her to walk on to Fiesole—we will follow in the carriage.

IRENE.

Oh, no, mamma—not walk! The girl looks painfully delicate.

MRS. STONEHAY.

My dear, I will *not* overload poor dumb animals.

WEAVER.

Excuse me, ma'am, but it's a terrible up-hill walk to Fiesole, and the sun is very hot at this time of the afternoon.

MRS. STONEHAY.

Thank you. The young lady is in my service.

WEAVER.

Oh, I beg pardon, ma'am. [WEAVER *goes.*]

IRENE.

Here she comes, mamma—little Leslie Brudenell. She is quite a woman.

MRS. STONEHAY.

I forget her entirely. We won't waste much time here; we'll just ascertain their position, take tea, and leave.

IRENE.

Oh, mamma, will you never admit that one may know people out of pure liking and nothing further!

MRS. STONEHAY.

My dear, do remember my creed! Men and women are sent into the world to help each other. Unfortunately I can help nobody, but it is none the less the solemn duty of others to help me.

[LESLIE, *looking very bright and happy, runs up the steps, meets* IRENE *and embraces her affectionately.*]

LESLIE.

Dear Irene!

IRENE.

You remember me?

LESLIE.

Remember you! You were kind to me at Helmstead.

IRENE.

I think you saw my mother once.

[LESLIE *bows to* MRS. STONEHAY, *and is joined by* DUNSTAN RENSHAW, *who has lost his dissipated look, and whose manner towards* LESLIE *is gentle, watchful, and tender.*]

LESLIE.

This is my husband.   [DUNSTAN *bows.*]

MRS. STONEHAY.

Very happy.

LESLIE.

You will let me give you some tea?

MRS. STONEHAY.

It seems barbarous to intrude upon people so recently married.

DUNSTAN RENSHAW.

On the contrary, Mrs. Stonehay, you may be able to console my wife in her first small grief.

MRS. STONEHAY.

So soon?

LESLIE.

Dunstan is obliged to leave me for two or three days.

DUNSTAN RENSHAW.

I am just off to Rome to furnish some lodgings we have taken there, in the Via Sistina. Poor Leslie was to have accompanied me, but Doctor Coldstream forbids the risk of a Roman hotel.

MRS. STONEHAY.

Leaving this delightful villa!

DUNSTAN RENSHAW.

Yes, the Villa Colobiano is delightful. At any rate Michael Angelo must have thought so at one time, when, in a moment of misapplied artistic ecstacy, he made his mark upon our wall.

LESLIE.

Oh, yes, we've suffered dreadfully. Dunstan didn't know when he took the Villa that it is honourably mentioned in Baedeker.

DUNSTAN RENSHAW.

The irrepressible Tourists have made our life a martyrdom. With guide-book, green spectacles, and sun-umbrella, they look for traces of Michael Angelo in every corner of the house.

LESLIE.

If we're dining they almost lift up the dish-covers.

DUNSTAN RENSHAW.

At first the servants hinted at a desire for seclusion on the part of a newly married couple.

LESLIE.

That made matters worse ; they wanted to see *us* then.

DUNSTAN RENSHAW.

Just as if we had been tatooed by Michael Angelo.

LESLIE.

[*Taking* IRENE's *hand.*] But it is such a relief to
see real friends. How did you discover us?
[IRENE *and* MRS. STONEHAY *look at each other.*]

IRENE.

We were driving out to Fiesole—and——

MRS. STONEHAY.

The coachman told us we ought to see Michael
Angelo's cartoon.

DUNSTAN RENSHAW.

Oh, of course — delighted — we're awfully
pleased——

LESLIE.

We didn't mean that we don't like showing the—
the——

MRS. STONEHAY.

What a magnificent view you command here!

LESLIE.

[*Whispering to* DUNSTAN.] Oh, darling, what a
muddle!

DUNSTAN RENSHAW.

Don't fret about it, sweetheart. I must go and
dress for my journey. You will drive with me to
the railway station?

LESLIE.

No, no. I couldn't part from you with people standing by. Not that I mean to cry.

DUNSTAN RENSHAW.

Cry! You must never shed tears. [*He kisses her fondly while the others are looking at the view.*] Why, there's old Wilfrid asleep. Make him help you with these Stonehenges.

[*He leaves her and she wakes* WILFRID.]

LESLIE.

Will! Will!

WILFRID BRUDENELL.

Eh! What is it? I think I must have dropped off to sleep.

LESLIE.

We've accidentally hurt some people's feelings. Assist me in being very nice to them.

WILFRID BRUDENELL.

Yes—but wait a minute. I'm not quite sure—where——

[*She drags* WILFRID *over to* MRS. STONEHAY *and* IRENE.]

LESLIE.

This is my brother, Wilfrid. [*Quietly to* WILFRID.] Rattle on, Will, dear. Wilfrid, you recollect meeting Miss Stonehay at Helmstead.

D

WILFRID BRUDENELL.

[*Only half awake, seizing* MRS. STONEHAY'S *hand.*]
O yes, I recollect you perfectly. You left school
some time ago, I suppose?

MRS. STONEHAY.

Yes—five-and-twenty years ago.

LESLIE.

Wilfrid! I want some more teacups. And brush
your hair. You've made it worse!

WILFRID BRUDENELL.

I'm afraid I am not quite awake.
[*He retires, the rest sit at the tea-table.*]

IRENE.

You make me feel quite old, Leslie—to see you
so much a woman.

LESLIE.

I am trying to be a woman, but I don't get on
very quickly.

IRENE.

Why try?

LESLIE.

Because I am ashamed that my husband's wife
should be so insignificant.

IRENE.

You seem very fond of him.

LESLIE.

Fond of him! Fond is a poor weak word. If I could realize my dearest desire I would be my husband's slave.

MRS. STONEHAY.

All new wives who have money and many domestic servants say that.

LESLIE.

Ah, but I would, truly. Do you know what it is to suffer keenly from over-kindness?

IRENE.

I thought that was a malady the Faculty had succeeded in stamping out.

LESLIE.

I suppose it lingers yet in some odd old-world corners; it is within the crumbling walls of this Villa, for instance. My husband is too devoted to me. I fear to have a wish because I know he cannot rest till it is gratified. If I look here, or there, his dear eyes imitate mine; if I rise, he starts up; if I walk on, he follows me. When he takes my hand he holds it as if it were a flower with a delicate bloom upon it; when he speaks to me he lowers his voice like one whispering into some rare shell that would break from too much sound. And all for one who is half a school-girl and half a woman, and so little of either.

[*A man is heard singing a characteristic Italian air to the accompaniment of a mandolin.*]

MRS. STONEHAY.

What's that?

[LESLIE *runs to the balustrade and waves her hand.*]

LESLIE.

That's Pietro Donigo, one of my husband's *protégés*. Dunstan wishes him to sing to me every day.

MRS. STONEHAY.

[*Sotto voce.*] Good gracious, what next! What is there in this girl to be sung at!

LESLIE.

Dun has been very good to Pietro, who is poor, with an old blind mother. Oh, he is good to everybody—good to everybody!

MRS. STONEHAY.

But, my dear Mrs. Renshaw, a wife ought not to be astonished at her husband's good-nature in the early days of their marriage. What else did you expect for the first month?

IRENE.

Hush, mamma dear; all Leslie means is that she is proud of her husband's goodness. What wife would not be?

LESLIE.

Yes, that is it—I am both proud and humble. Why, look! Directly we came here he sought out all the poor; in a few days they have learnt to bless his name, and when I pray for him I think I hear their chant echoing me. I tell you, sometimes

I hide myself away to shed tears of gratitude, and it's then that I think a woman's heart might be broken less easily by cruelty than by too much kindness!

MRS. STONEHAY.

[*To herself.*] This girl's parade of her model husband is insufferable ; it is time I ended it.

MRS. STONEHAY. [WILFRID *returns.*]

By the way, Mrs. Renshaw, I hope that out of your vast contentment you can spare some congratulations for my daughter.

IRENE.

No, no, mamma.

LESLIE.

Congratulations !

MRS. STONEHAY.

During our visit to Rome, Mrs. Renshaw, Irene has become most fortunately engaged.

LESLIE.

[*Embracing* IRENE.] To be married ?

IRENE.

Yes.

MRS. STONEHAY.

The combination of qualities possessed by Mrs. Renshaw's husband is rare. Nevertheless I think that some of the finest attributes of heart and mind are bestowed in an eminent degree upon Lord Dangars.

LESLIE.

Dear Irene, I hope you will be—oh, you *must* be, as happy as I am. Tell me about him. Wilfrid, point out San Croce to Mrs. Stonehay, and—and show her our little garden.

[WILFRID *escorts* MRS. STONEHAY *towards the garden.*]

MRS. STONEHAY.

[*To herself.*] The chit has no rank to boast about, at any rate.

LESLIE.

Go on. Do make me your confidante.

IRENE.

No, no.

LESLIE.

Lord Dangars, your mother said. Have I the name correctly? Lady Dangars!

IRENE.

Leslie—I—I can't talk about it.

LESLIE.

Can't talk about your sweetheart?

IRENE.

Hush! Lord Dangars is simply a man who wishes to marry me and whom my mother wishes me to marry. We are poor and she has her ambitions; there you have two volumes of a three-volume novel.

LESLIE.

You don't—love him?

IRENE.

Love him !

LESLIE.

Then you mustn't do this. Dear, can't I help you?

IRENE.

You help me! Child, my small corner in the world is hewn out of stone ; there's not a path there that it would not bruise your little feet to tread.

MRS. STONEHAY.

[*To* WILFRID.] I am in ecstacy! The moment Lord Dangars arrives in Florence I shall bring him to the Villa Colobiano.

WILFRID BRUDENELL.

This is the way to the garden.

MRS. STONEHAY.

[*Watching* LESLIE *and* IRENE.] I thought so. We shall not be patronized by Mrs. Renshaw again.
   [WILFRID *and* MRS. STONEHAY *go down the garden steps.*]

LESLIE.

But perhaps you will learn to love Lord Dangars. Is he young?

IRENE.

Sufficiently so to escape being taken for my— grandfather.

LESLIE.

Handsome?

IRENE.

There is no accepted standard for man's beauty.

LESLIE.

Oh, be more serious. Is he a bachelor or a widower?

IRENE.

Neither.

LESLIE.

Neither?

IRENE.

Lord Dangars is a *divorcé*.

LESLIE.

A *divorcé?* At least, then, he deserves your pity.

IRENE.

For what?

LESLIE.

For his sorrow. He must have suffered.

IRENE.

No, it was scarcely Lord Dangars who suffered.

LESLIE.

[*Shrinking from* IRENE.] *His wife?*

IRENE.

Yes.

LESLIE.

And you will—marry him! Oh! For shame, Irene!

IRENE.

Leslie!

LESLIE.

I can't think of it !

IRENE.

Be silent !   I have the world upon my side—what is your girl's voice against the world !   I shall have money and a title—I shall have satisfied my mother at last.   Why should you make it harder for me by even a word ?

LESLIE.

I want to save you from sharing this man's hideous disgrace.

IRENE.

Oh, the world has a short memory for a man's disgrace.   It is only with women that it lays down scandal, as it lays down wine, to ripen and mature.

LESLIE.

But *you* will not forget ; you will die under the burden of your husband's past.

IRENE.

I ! oh, no !   What is a man's past to the woman who marries him !

LESLIE.

It is her pride or her shame, the jewel she wears upon her brow or the mud which clings to her skirts !   It is her light or her darkness ; her life or her death !

IRENE.

You're too young a wife to lecture me like this! The only difference between me and other women will be that Lord Dangars's story is public and their husband's vices are unrevealed!

LESLIE.

That is not true! You have no right to defend yourself in that way.

IRENE.

It *is* true! What woman who doesn't wish to be lied to would ask her husband to unfold the record of his life of—liberty?

LESLIE.

What woman would——! *I* would!

IRENE.

Simpleton!

LESLIE.

A thousand times, I would! Oh, under my dear husband's roof how dare you think so cruelly of good men!

[*She runs to* DUNSTAN *as he enters dressed for travelling.*]

MRS. STONEHAY.

[*Rejoining them with* WILFRID.] Irene, we are forgetting our drive to Fiesole.

DUNSTAN RENSHAW.

[*To* LESLIE.] What's the matter? Have I been away too long?

LESLIE.

It is always too long when you are away.

Mrs. Stonehay.

Good-bye, dear Mrs. Renshaw.

Leslie.

[*Distantly.*] Good-bye.

Mrs. Stonehay.

My dear Mr. Renshaw, everything here is too charming !

Irene.

[*To* Leslie.] Forgive me. My life has made me bitter. Sometimes I am nearly mad.

Leslie.

Come and see me again, Irene. When you know my husband better you will realize how little your world has taught you. [Leslie *kisses* Irene.]

Mrs. Stonehay.

Irene, I believe I can see that obstinate young woman sitting down in a vineyard—not a quarter of a mile from this house yet. There is a limit even to my forbearance.
[Wilfrid, Mrs. Stonehay, *and* Irene *go out.* Leslie *gives* Dunstan *a cup of tea.*]

Leslie.

The stirrup cup.

Dunstan Renshaw.

You will think of me in the toils of the Roman furniture and *bric-à-brac* dealers, won't you ?

LESLIE.

Think of you !

DUNSTAN RENSHAW.

I shall fight through the worry of it in a couple of days and then—there will be the first home of our own making. Just imagine when we skip up the stone stairs in the Via Sistina and I throw open the door——

LESLIE.

Our own door !

DUNSTAN RENSHAW.

Our own door—and we see our own chairs and tables, our own pictures, our own——

LESLIE. [*He pauses suddenly.*]

Dun ! Dun, dear ?

DUNSTAN RENSHAW.

This separating, even for a day or two, is a heavy-hearted business.

LESLIE.

It shall always be so, dear, always.

DUNSTAN RENSHAW.

While I'm gone you'll not forget the lame girl in the Via Vellutini—or Pietro's old mother——?

LESLIE.

No, dear, no.

DUNSTAN RENSHAW.

And—and double the allowance to those little children we helped yesterday.

LESLIE.

If you wish it ; but the father is working here now in our garden——

DUNSTAN RENSHAW.

Never mind—double it, treble it ! I don't spend enough, half enough, in conscience money.

LESLIE.

Conscience money !

DUNSTAN RENSHAW.

That is the name I give my little charities.

LESLIE.

Do you call all charity conscience money ?

DUNSTAN RENSHAW.

No. But, Leslie, no man is good enough for a good woman, and so I'm trying to buy my right to possess you——

LESLIE.

To possess *me !* Worthless me !

DUNSTAN RENSHAW.

My right to your love and—your esteem.

LESLIE.

Oh, Dun, you are sad ! As if anything in life could rob you of my worship.

DUNSTAN RENSHAW.

Nothing that could happen ?

LESLIE.

Husband, what *could* happen !

[HUGH MURRAY *enters unseen by* LESLIE, *but* DUNSTAN *stares at him, as if in terror.*]

DUNSTAN RENSHAW.

Murray !

HUGH MURRAY.

Pardon me. Wilfrid told me to——

LESLIE.

Mr. Murray ! Oh, dear Mr. Murray !

[*She takes his hands.*]

WILFRID.

[*Joining them.*] The very last man we expected at the Villa Colobiano ! And, what do you think, Dunstan—he hasn't come to see the old fresco!

LESLIE.

Dunstan !

[HUGH *and* DUNSTAN *look significantly at* LESLIE, *and then shake hands.*]

DUNSTAN RENSHAW.

As Wilfrid says, you are the last man we looked to see in Florence.

LESLIE.

But, oh, so welcome !

HUGH MURRAY.

You must not, I'm sorry to say, consider this the visit of a friend, Mr. Renshaw.

LESLIE.

Have you travelled so many miles to talk only about business?

HUGH MURRAY.

Yes.

LESLIE.

Ah, be a friend first and let the business wait.

HUGH MURRAY.

I leave here to-night, and I must speak to Mr. Renshaw without delay.

DUNSTAN RENSHAW.

I can give you only five minutes. Leslie.

LESLIE.

I shall make a nosegay for my dear, and bring it when the five minutes are gone. [*Tenderly to* DUNSTAN.] You have made me forget there is anything in the world called Business.

[*She follows* WILFRID *down the garden steps.* DUNSTAN *watches her for a moment, then faces* HUGH.]

DUNSTAN RENSHAW.

Do you come here, may I ask, to take up our acquaintance at the point where it was broken a month ago?

HUGH MURRAY.

I regret that I must do so.

DUNSTAN RENSHAW.

As a friend—or as an enemy?

HUGH MURRAY.

Neither—as a man who feels he has a duty to follow, and who will follow it.

DUNSTAN RENSHAW.

What do you consider your duty?

HUGH MURRAY.

This. There is no need to remind you of my knowledge of the doings of Mr. Lawrence Kenward.

DUNSTAN RENSHAW.

Murray!

HUGH MURRAY.

I did not use your name.

DUNSTAN RENSHAW.

You know the poor creature who—you know her?

HUGH MURRAY.

She came to me, in ignorance of my association with you, on the very day, at the very moment, of your marriage.

DUNSTAN RENSHAW.

What did she want of you?

HUGH MURRAY.

My aid in searching for her betrayer.

DUNSTAN RENSHAW.

Don't tell me she is the girl whom my wife and her brother encountered at the railway station in London!

HUGH MURRAY.

She is the girl.

DUNSTAN RENSHAW.

That's fatality—fatality.

HUGH MURRAY.

Before she had been with me ten minutes, I discovered the actual identity of the man Kenward.

DUNSTAN RENSHAW.

Oh!

HUGH MURRAY.

And I deliberately and dishonestly concealed my knowledge from her.

DUNSTAN RENSHAW.

For *my* sake?

HUGH MURRAY.

No—for the sake of the child you had made your wife.

DUNSTAN RENSHAW.

My wife. Janet Preece can have her revenge now. My wife—my wife.

HUGH MURRAY.

The girl left me on your marriage morning upon the understanding that I would write to her.

DUNSTAN RENSHAW.

Yes.

HUGH MURRAY.

I did write, the day following, to an address she

E

gave me, in the country.　I wrote instructing her to take no steps till she heard from me *a month thence.*

DUNSTAN RENSHAW.

That is a month ago !

HUGH MURRAY.

Exactly a month ago.

DUNSTAN RENSHAW.

What do you intend to do now ?

HUGH MURRAY.

Write to her once more, confessing that I have done nothing, and intend to do nothing, to aid her.

DUNSTAN RENSHAW.

Oh, Murray !

HUGH MURRAY.

Man, don't thank me !　For the sake of one poor creature, your wife, I have been dishonest to another poor creature, your broken plaything !　For one month I have lied for you in act and in spirit.　In the race between you and your victim I have given the strong man a month's start ; to her a month of suspense, to you a month of thoughtless happiness. You have taken it, enjoyed it, steeped yourself to the lips in it ; and now, from this day, you play the game of your life without a confederate.　Our paths divide !

DUNSTAN RENSHAW.

Murray !　Listen to me !　You are the only man who may have it in his power to help me !

HUGH MURRAY.

I have done so—for a month.

DUNSTAN RENSHAW.

I don't ask you to pity the girl I have ill-used or the girl I have married—that you must do. But, wretch that I am, you might do a greater injustice than to pity me.

HUGH MURRAY.

Pity *you!*

DUNSTAN RENSHAW.

Murray, a month ago I married this child. Perhaps, then, I was really in love with her; I hardly know, for loving had been to me like a tune a man hums for a day and can't recall a week afterwards. But this I *do* know—I have grown to love her now with my whole soul!

HUGH MURRAY.

[*Contemptuously.*] Oh!

DUNSTAN RENSHAW.

I married her, as it were, in darkness; she seemed to take me by the hand and to lead me out into the light. Murray, the companionship of this pure woman is a revelation of life to me! I tell you there are times when she stands before me that I am like a man dazzled and can scarcely look at her without shading my eyes. But *you* know—because you read my future—*you* know what my existence has become! The Past has overtaken me! I am in deadly fear! I dread the visit of a stranger, or the sight of strange handwriting, and in my sleep I dream that I am muttering into her ear the truth against myself! And, oh, Murray, there is one thing more that is the rack to me and yet a delight, a paradise and yet a torment, a curse and yet a blessing, my wife—God help me!—my wife thinks me—Good!

LESLIE.

[*In the garden below.*] Dunstan! Dunstan!

HUGH MURRAY.

Your wife! Be quick! Tell me—how can I help you?

DUNSTAN RENSHAW.

Ah, Murray!

HUGH MURRAY.

For her sake—for her sake!

DUNSTAN RENSHAW.

The moment you reach London send for Janet Preece—tell her the truth—entreat her to be silent. Tell her I will do all in my power to atone if she will be but silent—only silent—silent!

LESLIE.

[*From the garden.*] Dunstan! The five minutes are gone.

[LESLIE *runs on carrying some flowers.* WILFRID *follows, leisurely, smoking a cigarette.*]

LESLIE.

Have I come back a minute too soon? [*To* DUNSTAN.] You have had bad news; ah, don't send me away again! You are troubled.

DUNSTAN RENSHAW.

Why, of course I am troubled.

LESLIE.

About nothing worse than leaving me?

DUNSTAN RENSHAW.

Isn't that bad enough?

LESLIE.

[*Giving him a bunch of flowers.*] For you. [*To* HUGH.] Is it unbusiness-like to give you a flower?

HUGH MURRAY.

Thank you.

[WEAVER *enters dressed for travelling.*]

WEAVER.

The carriage is at the door, sir.

DUNSTAN RENSHAW.

Send it round to the gate. I will walk with Mrs. Renshaw through the garden.

[WEAVER *retires.*]

LESLIE.

Wilfrid is here to amuse you, Mr. Murray, if I am poor company. Must you leave us too?

HUGH MURRAY.

Thank you—yes. I turn my face homeward to-night.

DUNSTAN RENSHAW.

I have something more to say to Murray. [*To* HUGH.] Will you drive down with me?

[HUGH *assents silently.*]

DUNSTAN RENSHAW.

[*Pointing into the distance.*] Leslie, when the carriage gets to that little rise stand here and beckon to me till I am out of sight.

LESLIE.

Beckon to you?

DUNSTAN RENSHAW.

Yes, I want to remember it while we are apart as the last sign you made me—beckoning me to return.   [*They go down the steps together.*]

HUGH MURRAY.

Wilfrid, don't ever tell her—your sister—that I asked you this. She is—quite happy?

WILFRID BRUDENELL.

Oh, she's awfully happy. But, I say, isn't she a lucky girl?

HUGH MURRAY.

Yes. Why?

WILFRID BRUDENELL.

To have the best fellow in the world for her husband.

HUGH MURRAY.

Look—they're waiting for me. Good-bye.

WILFRID BRUDENELL.

Good-bye. [*He shakes hands with* HUGH, *who descends the steps.*] No, I sha'n't assist at Dun's departure. I'm afraid Les will cry, and I can't bear to see a girl cry; it makes me feel so dreadfully queer in the chest. Dun is saying good-bye to her now. Oh, well now, she is a brick! She's rolled her handkerchief into a ball and put it in her pocket. There's Murray. In he gets! Away they go! Poor Leslie's head is drooping. Confound it, she's taking out her handkerchief! I can't stand it.

[PRISCILLA *enters from the villa, crying.*]

PRISCILLA.

Mr. Wilfrid.

WILFRID BRUDENELL.

Well? Oh, now, what are *you* crying about?

PRISCILLA.

The young person, sir, who was with the two ladies who came to see our cartoon, has been sent back on foot, and she's downstairs begging for a morsel of water; and, oh, Mr. Wilfrid, the poor thing looks so weak and ill!

WILFRID BRUDENELL.

Ill! Where is she?
[*He goes into the villa, as* LESLIE *slowly ascends the garden steps. The serenade is heard again.*]

LESLIE.

No, Pietro mustn't sing to me while he is gone. My home shall never be bright and cheerful when its dear master is away.

WILFRID BRUDENELL.

[*From the house.*]   Leslie!   Leslie!

LESLIE.

Will?   [WILFRID *comes from the villa with* JANET PREECE, *who looks weary and feeble.* [*Taking* JANET'S *hand.*]   Oh!   Wilfrid!

WILFRID BRUDENELL.

It's our little friend of the London railway station!

JANET PREECE.

No, no—I am only Mrs. Stonehay's servant—little better.   She has threatened to send me away, because she says I am self-willed and won't obey her. But I—I can't walk; I'm not over-strong.   What shall I do!
> [*She falls back fainting;* WILFRID *catches her in his arms.* LESLIE *kneels beside her, loosening the strings of her bonnet.*]

LESLIE.

Oh, poor girl!   Why, she is no older than I.   Ah, Will, she sha'n't want a shelter!   Priscilla!   Priscilla!

WILFRID BRUDENELL.

Priscilla!

LESLIE.

`Oh! the carriage! [*She runs quickly to the balustrade and looks out into the distance.*] It's there! [*She beckons thrice.*] Dunstan—come back to me! Come back to me!

END OF THE SECOND ACT.

THE THIRD ACT.

THE END OF THE HONEYMOON.

The scene is still the RENSHAWS' *Florentine villa.* JANET
PREECE *is lying upon a sofa, and* WILFRID *is
sitting on a footstool by her side reading to her.*

WILFRID BRUDENELL.

Miss Preece, I hope you're tired of my reading.

JANET PREECE.

Why?

WILFRID BRUDENELL.

Because you've heard all that Galignani has to
remark.

JANET PREECE.

I'm afraid I haven't heard much.

WILFRID BRUDENELL.

Not heard much! oh!

JANET PREECE.

Not much of Galignani. I've never been read to
before, and I only know that your kind voice has
been rising and falling and rising and falling, and
all for me. I didn't want to hear the words.

WILFRID BRUDENELL.

By Jove ! You're quite yourself this morning, aren't you ?

JANET PREECE.

No—not myself. I feel so happy. But I am dreadfully puzzled. Tell me—have I been very ill ?

WILFRID BRUDENELL.

[*Holding her hand.*] Just near enough to brain fever to be able to say " How do you do ? " to it and go off in another direction.

JANET PREECE.

Have I been ill long ?

WILFRID BRUDENELL.

Long enough to make me—to make us desperately anxious.

JANET PREECE.

How long is that ?

WILFRID BRUDENELL.

Three days.

JANET PREECE.

Three days—three days. How strange to have lost three days out of one's life ! I seem to have died and to have come into a beautiful new world.

WILFRID BRUDENELL.

That's a great compliment to the Villa Colobiano and its mistress.

JANET PREECE.

Ah, she is the Angel of my new world !

WILFRID BRUDENELL.

One angel is very little to do all the work of a beautiful new world.

[JANET *timidly withdraws her hand.*]

JANET PREECE.

Oh, she has her brother to help her, of course.

[LESLIE *enters, and* JANET *embraces her.*]

LESLIE.

The post brought me a letter from my dear one—my husband—and I hid myself away to read it.

WILFRID BRUDENELL.

When does Dun start for home, Les?

LESLIE.

I don't know; this was written the day before yesterday.

JANET PREECE.

Your husband? You—you are married?

LESLIE.

Married! Ah, I forget that my poor invalid knows nothing about her nurse. Let me tell you. I mustn't blame you for not guessing it; but I am that exceedingly important person, a newly-married lady. I am Mrs. Renshaw.

JANET PREECE.

[*Taking* LESLIE'S *hand.*] Mrs.—Renshaw. I shall say the name to myself over and over again that I may seem to have known you longer. Mrs.—Renshaw.

LESLIE.

Yes, and my husband is in Rome preparing our first real home. You will see him soon—oh, I hope very soon.

JANET PREECE.

I should like to see one who is so precious to you, of course—only——

LESLIE.

Only—what?

JANET PREECE.

Only I know that when your dear companion comes back I shall lose you.

LESLIE.

Hush, hush! You mustn't distress yourself; you will be ill again.

JANET PREECE.

I would be ill again, gladly, if I could see your face constantly bending over me as I have seen it for the last three days. Oh, Mrs. Renshaw, why have you been so good to me, a stranger?

WILFRID BRUDENELL.

I say, Leslie, aren't Dun's letters furious about Mrs. Stonehay's bad behaviour?

JANET PREECE.

Mrs. Stonehay! I can't go back to her! Oh, don't send me back to Mrs. Stonehay! Oh, don't, please don't!

LESLIE.

No, dear, no—of course not. [*To* WILFRID.] Why,
I haven't written a word to Dun about our little visitor and Mrs. Stonehay's resentment at our sheltering her. If I had, the dear fellow would have flown
home to fight my battles for me, and left his business unfinished. I know Dun.

JANET PREECE.

Mrs. Stonehay's resentment at your giving me
shelter! Oh, why should she be so cruel to me!

LESLIE.

Hush, dear—it is Mrs. Stonehay's nature to be
jealous and arrogant. When she discovered that
her dependent, as she called you, was installed here
as my friend, she indignantly reproached me for en-
ticing you from her service.

WILFRID BRUDENELL.

I never saw a woman so angry. I had the honour
of bowing her out at the front door, and she de-
clared she shook the dust of the Villa Colobiano
from her feet ; luckily, it was only a figure of speech,
for her feet are very large.

[PRISCILLA *enters.*]

PRISCILLA.

Miss Stonehay is here, ma'am.

[PRISCILLA *retires.*]

JANET PREECE.

Oh, Mrs. Renshaw!

LESLIE.

Don't be alarmed, Janet. You don't know that during the last three days the face you have seen bending over you has often been poor Irene's.

[IRENE *enters, and appears agitated.*]

LESLIE.

Irene. You are trembling—there is some trouble?

IRENE.

[*Quietly to* LESLIE.] Yes—I've come to tell you. Janet, I am glad to see you almost well again. Don't you believe me?

JANET PREECE.

[*Shrinking from her.*] Yes—I—I am better.

IRENE.

Ah, don't be frightened of me—not of *me !* Janet !
[JANET *looks at* IRENE, *then goes to her.*]

IRENE.

[*Kissing* JANET.] Thank you. [*Giving* LESLIE *a letter.*] A letter, Leslie.

LESLIE.

From your mother?

IRENE.

From my mother. Read it.

LESLIE.

[*As she reads.*] Oh—oh ! Irene, do you guess the drift of this?

IRENE.

Better than you do, Leslie. It is a humble apology from Mrs. Stonehay for her unintentional rudeness upon misunderstanding the motive of Mrs. Renshaw's extreme kindness to poor Miss Preece.

LESLIE.

Yes, it is an apology.

IRENE.

Followed by an entreaty that Mrs. Renshaw will permit Mrs. Stonehay to call at the Villa Colobiano immediately to make peace in person.
[WILFRID *and* JANET *go down into the garden.*]

LESLIE.

You know the letter almost word for word.

IRENE.

I know my mother better day by day. Leslie, you don't see what that means?

LESLIE.

That your mother is sorry.

IRENE.

No — it means that she has just heard from Lord Dangars that he is an old and intimate friend of your husband's, and that they chanced to come together again two days ago in Rome.

LESLIE.

I am grieved to pain you, Irene, but I am sure

that my husband can't be aware of the true character of Lord Dangars.

IRENE.

Possibly not, but my mother sees that Lord Dangars may hear of her conduct through Mr. Renshaw, and is therefore anxious to conciliate you without delay.

LESLIE.

Oh! [*She tears* MRS. STONEHAY's *letter into pieces.*]

IRENE.

Oh, Leslie, the meanness of my life is crushing me! I can't be faithful to my mother, and yet I loathe myself for being a traitor to her. I seem to bring a worldly taint even into your home, and yet your home is so sweet and pure to me that I haven't the courage to shut myself out of it. How you must despise me!

[WEAVER *enters.*]

LESLIE.

Weaver!

WEAVER.

I beg your pardon, ma'am; I wasn't aware you were engaged.

LESLIE.

Why have you left your master in Rome? He is —well?

WEAVER.

Quite, ma'am. I haven't left the master in Rome; we got back to Florence this morning.

F

LESLIE.

He is in Florence !

WEAVER.

Master finished his business in Rome a little sooner than he expected, and we made a rush, ma'am, for the night train. Getting in so very early this morning, master thought it best to go to the *Hôtel de la Paix* for an hour or two.

LESLIE.

Thought it best to go to the *Hôtel de la Paix!* Oh, there must be some reason !

WEAVER.

[*Handing a letter to* LESLIE.] The reason is, ma'am, that master is bringing a visitor home with him and didn't think it right to take you quite unprepared.

LESLIE.

A visitor?

WEAVER.

Yes, ma'am—Lord Dangars.

LESLIE.

Lord Dangars here ! Oh ! Dunstan, Dunstan !

IRENE.

[*To herself.*] So soon—so soon ; so short a respite ! [WILFRID *and* JANET *come up the steps from the garden.*]

LESLIE.

[*To herself as she reads the letter.*] Ah, I knew it ! My poor Dun, to be victimized by such a companion-

ship. I quite understand, Weaver. Mr. Renshaw
will be here almost directly?

WEAVER.

He and his lordship were at breakfast when I left,
ma'am; in less than half-an-hour, I should say.

LESLIE.

Tell the servants. [WEAVER *goes out.*]

IRENE.

Leslie, the thought that you are to be thrown into
the society of this man is unendurable to me.

LESLIE.

And yet you are speaking of the man you are
going to marry.

IRENE.

Certainly, but by my marriage I hope to lose
much of his society. But you—oh, your husband
is to blame, to blame !

LESLIE.

Hush, Irene! You do Mr. Renshaw an injustice.
Look. [*She hands* IRENE DUNSTAN'S *letter.*] Will,
Dun has come back! Janet, be glad for my sake!

IRENE.

[*Reading the letter.*] "Dear One. Weaver will
explain my mode of arrival. Dangars I once knew
fairly well, and somehow he won't be shaken off now.
As there appears to be an engagement between him
and your friend Miss Stonehay I have asked him

to be our guest for a couple of days, thinking you may consider it a kindness to her; but please don't extend the term, as he is not quite the man I wish my wife to count among her acquaintances."

[JANET *and* WILFRID *stroll away*.]

LESLIE.

[*To herself.*] My husband home again — home again—home again! But, oh, why hasn't he come back to me alone!

IRENE.

Leslie, I perceive I *have* done Mr. Renshaw an injustice. But surely you had some further motive in sharing with me the privilege of enjoying Mr. Renshaw's estimate of the gentleman who is to be my husband?

LESLIE.

Yes, I had. I *will* convince you of the contempt in which honest men hold such as Lord Dangars.

IRENE.

[*Crushing the letter in her hand.*] Thank you— I—— Leslie! you are right—save me—save me!

LESLIE.

Irene !

IRENE.

I knew that my next meeting with Lord Dangars could not be long delayed, and I taught myself to think of it coldly and callously. But, now that the moment has come, and I am to lay my hand in his and look him in the face—a woman willing to sell herself—every nerve in my body is on fire with the shame of it and I can't, I can't fall so utterly!

LESLIE.

Dear Irene, I knew I should save you !

IRENE.

Ah, but can you ? I am such a coward ; I haven't the courage of your good instincts. If you don't help me I shall falter and be lost !

LESLIE.

But I can help you. *I* will make an appeal to your mother.

IRENE.

That's hopeless, hopeless !

LESLIE.

Then I will face Lord Dangars himself.

IRENE.

You !

LESLIE.

Yes, with my husband. Ah, Irene, there are good men still to fight the battles of weak women, and I promise you my dear husband's aid.

[WILFRID *and* JANET *re-appear, talking earnestly.*]

IRENE.

Hush !

LESLIE.

[*Quietly to* IRENE.] Go back to your mother and tell her I will see her in answer to her letter.

[LESLIE *and* IRENE *go into the villa.*]

JANET PREECE.

[*To* WILFRID.] No, no, please. don't speak to me like that! I mustn't listen to you, indeed I mustn't.

WILFRID BRUDENELL.

I never thought I should hurt you by what I've said. What I was foolish enough to think was—that perhaps you—didn't dislike me.

JANET PREECE.

Dislike you! Why, there's no book in the world that's long enough, and no poetry ever written that's sweet enough, to match what I think, but can't say, in gratitude to you and Mrs. Renshaw.

WILFRID BRUDENELL.

Ah, we don't want you to thank us, Janet—unless it's by a tinge of colour in your white face. You make me feel how mean I've been to ask for your love.

JANET PREECE.

Oh, stop, stop! I can't bear you to say such a thing.

WILFRID BRUDENELL.

I've no right to press you for the reason you can't love me.

JANET PREECE.

No, no—don't, don't!

WILFRID BRUDENELL.

I can only guess what's in your mind. Is it that we're such new friends to talk of love and marriage? Because, Janet, if we know each other for years I

can never alter the truth, that it took only a minute
to fall in love with you.

JANET PREECE.

No, it isn't that you're a new friend ; for the matter o' that, after Mrs. Renshaw, you're my only
friend.   It isn't that—it isn't that.

WILFRID BRUDENELL.

Then, if we're your only friends, at least I know
that you don't love any other——

JANET PREECE.

[*Starting up and hiding her face from him.*]   Any
other !

WILFRID BRUDENELL.

Any other—man.

JANET PREECE.

No—no .   I don't—I don't love any other man.

WILFRID BRUDENELL.

And yet you can't love *me*.   I'm answered.   Ah,
Janet, a man who isn't loved had better never seek
the reason, or if he does he should look for it—in
himself.   My brother-in-law will be home in a few
minutes and I can very well be spared here.   So
there's one thing I beg of you, that you won't let
this—stupidity of mine shorten your stay at the
Villa Colobiano.

JANET PREECE.

[*Bursting into tears.*]   I can't bear it !   My heart
will break !

WILFRID BRUDENELL.

You seemed in bitter trouble when we first met;

don't leave us till we have helped to make life easier for you.

JANET PREECE.

Oh, if we never had met—if we never had met!

WILFRID BRUDENELL.

Why, I've done nothing but love you, Janet. Come, you're not cruel enough to wish you had never seen me?

JANET PREECE.

Ah, no! No! Believe me, the only happiness for such as I is in such wretchedness as this. Bid me good-bye—I am going.

WILFRID BRUDENELL.

No!

JANET PREECE.

Let me steal away quietly. Tell your sister that I pray God to bless her, her husband, and her children when they come to make her life perfect; say I am only a poor creature never worth the love I've stolen from you both, but that my thoughts will be only of you and her till I die.

WILFRID BRUDENELL.

No, you must not leave the house till you have seen Leslie.

JANET PREECE.

Don't keep me here! If I see her again I must tell her why I run away from the one sweet prospect my life has given me!

WILFRID BRUDENELL.

You *do* love me then ! You *do* love me !

[*He draws her to him, but she breaks away with a low
cry as* LESLIE *enters.*]

JANET PREECE.

Let me go ! let me go !

LESLIE.

Janet !

JANET PREECE.

[*To* LESLIE *in a low whisper.*] Mrs. Renshaw !
You don't know what a base, wicked girl you are
sheltering ! I'm not fit to be in your house ! Oh,
I'll tell you—I'll tell you !

WILFRID BRUDENELL.

Leslie, there have been no secrets between us
ever, and there's a promise that there never shall be
any.

LESLIE.

Will ?

WILFRID BRUDENELL.

I—I have told Janet that I love her, and I have
asked her to be my wife. But Janet is in some distress and wishes to leave us. So, Les, I want you
to do me a service.

LESLIE.

What service, brother dear ?

WILFRID BRUDENELL.

I want you to help her—and me.

[*He leaves them together.*]

LESLIE.

Janet! Janet Preece. I love my brother very dearly, and long ago I determined that the moment his heart went out to a good girl I would call her my sister without a murmur. But you have said something to me which has—frightened me. Oh, Janet, what is it that's wrong—what is it that's wrong? [JANET *kneels humbly at* LESLIE'S *feet.*] Why do you kneel, Janet?

JANET PREECE.

Because it's my place in the world for evermore; because I'm of no more worth than the clod of earth you turn aside with your foot; because the time has been when I was one of the tempted and not one of the strong.

LESLIE.

[*Turning away.*] Oh, Janet, Janet.

JANET PREECE.

When I found that your brother loved me I wanted to run away without the dreadful shame of confessing the truth to you. But I'm a little happier for having told you, and I'll go out of your house now quickly and quietly, and you'll never see me nor hear of me again. [*Kissing the edge of* LESLIE'S *dress.*] Good-bye—my dear. Good-bye, oh my dear, my dear.   [*She rises, and is about to go.*]

LESLIE.

No, no! Stop! What you have told me seems to have stunned me. I—I can't realize it yet.

JANET PREECE.

Don't try to—it's better you should never realize it.

LESLIE.

A few minutes ago you and I were like simple girls; now we have suddenly become sad grown women. Will—my poor Will! What shall I do?

JANET PREECE.

Nothing but let me go.

LESLIE.

Let you go! You have come into my life now, and your weakness and loneliness make it my task to protect you. Put on your hat—quickly. [JANET *hesitates.*] Quickly! Throw that shawl over your shoulders. [JANET *obediently puts on the hat and shawl.* LESLIE *begins writing hurriedly at the table.*] You mustn't re-enter this house; you and my brother must never meet again. My poor brother! I am going o send you to a friend who will gladly render me a service. This afternoon I will come to you. "The Villa Lotta, Viale dei Colli." Are you ready?

JANET PREECE.

Yes.

LESLIE.

Present this—and here, here is some money.
Come, we will go through the garden.

[*They go together to the garden steps.   Suddenly*
JANET *utters a cry of horror.*]

LESLIE.

Janet !

JANET PREECE.

[*Dragging* LESLIE *from the steps.*]   Come away—
come away !   Look there !   Look there !

LESLIE.

[*Looking into the garden.*]   My husband and
Lord Dangars.

JANET PREECE.

It's the man—the man !

LESLIE.

The man !   Lord Dangars !

JANET PREECE.

He lied to me ; I have never known his true name
till now.   That's the man who called himself Lawrence Kenward.

LESLIE.

Great Heavens !   They are coming this way into
the house.

JANET PREECE.

Ah, hide me, hide me !   I haven't the courage to
meet him.   Ah, hide me !

[*She staggers to the sofa and sinks down beside
it.*]

LESLIE.

Janet!

[LESLIE *crouches down by* JANET *and puts her arms round her protectingly, as* DUNSTAN REN-SHAW *and* LORD DANGARS *ascend the steps.*]

LORD DANGARS.

Phew! I'm smothered with dust; you would walk.

DUNSTAN RENSHAW.

I'm very sorry. Shall we restore the perfection of our appearance before looking for Mrs. Renshaw? [*They go into the villa.*]

LESLIE.

Janet! Do you know that this is the man to whom Irene Stonehay is engaged to be married?

JANET PREECE.

I—I've heard them speak of him; I never suspected who he was. Heaven pity her! He'll kill her, body and soul.

LESLIE.

No, no. It is you who must help me to save her.

JANET PREECE.

I!

LESLIE.

You must. If you do your utmost to rescue this weak woman from the dreadful life that is before her you'll do something to make you happier in the future.

JANET PREECE.

What can I do! I couldn't shame him.

LESLIE.

But you could shame her mother—you could drive any remaining feeling of irresolution from this poor girl's mind.

JANET PREECE.

They wouldn't believe me ; why should they?

LESLIE.

Then, if they doubt you, will you face this miserable libertine before their eyes?

JANET PREECE.

Ah, no, no ! For months I've been seeking him to beg him to make reparation to me, but now that I've found him I want to put miles between us, for I feel I'd rather go down to my grave what I am than live what he could make me !

[PRISCILLA *enters.*]

PRISCILLA.

Mrs. Stonehay and Miss Stonehay are here, ma'am.

JANET PREECE.

Oh !

LESLIE.

I'll see them.   [PRISCILLA *retires.*]

JANET PREECE.

Let me go—give me leave to go.

LESLIE.

You are free to go, Janet—go.   But you are going from your duty.

JANET PREECE.

My duty—my duty. If *he* came to hear of it,
would he think a little better of me for it?

LESLIE.

He?

JANET PREECE.

Wilfrid—your brother.

LESLIE.

I think he would.

JANET PREECE.

I'll stay. I'll try and do my duty.

[*She sinks upon the sofa as* MRS. STONEHAY *and* IRENE
enter. MRS. STONEHAY *advances to* LESLIE *with
outstretched hands.*]

MRS. STONEHAY.

My dear Mrs. Renshaw!

LESLIE.

[*Coldly.*] Mrs. Stonehay.

MRS. STONEHAY.

Dear child, what can I say to you in reference to
our—misunderstanding, shall I call it?

LESLIE.

Say nothing, please, nothing.

MRS. STONEHAY.

We will say nothing. The passing ill-humours of
a crochetty but not unamiable old woman are best
forgotten. Ah, my dear, remember I am about to
lose my daughter. But I have yet to make my

peace with our little friend here. You have been indisposed, my poor Janet? Let it be a lesson to you—never mistake firmness for unkindness. Don't stand, in your weak state. [JANET *sinks back upon the sofa.*] I am positively in ecstasies, dear Mrs. Renshaw, to learn that Lord Dangars is to be a guest at the Villa Colobiano.

LESLIE.

To my surprise I find that my husband and this gentleman are acquainted.

MRS. STONEHAY.

Are old and close friends. And you weren't aware of it! Delightful!

LESLIE.

I say again I am *surprised.*

MRS. STONEHAY.

Naturally. You will like Dangars. He has suffered, poor fellow, but he has come out of the furnace a very refined metal.

LESLIE.

My husband—knowing Lord Dangars, I venture to think, but slightly—has indeed invited him to this house.

MRS. STONEHAY.

Charming! It brings us all so closely together. Will Lord Dangars, may I ask, remain with you very long?

LESLIE.

No.

MRS. STONEHAY.

No?

LESLIE.

Because, Mrs. Stonehay, I cannot, I regret to say, consent to receive Lord Dangars.

MRS. STONEHAY.

I confess I don't understand. Your husband's friend——

LESLIE.

No, Mrs. Stonehay ; my husband has only to know Lord Dangars as thoroughly as I do to consider him an unfit companion for any reputable man or woman.

MRS. STONEHAY.

Do you forget that you are speaking of one who is to be my daughter's husband? Irene! are you dumb?

[LESLIE *turns to* IRENE, *who is sitting with her head bowed and her hands clasped.*]

LESLIE.

Irene! Irene!
[IRENE *rises, supporting herself by the table.*]

IRENE.

Mother—don't ask me to marry Lord Dangars! Oh, don't make me do that—don't make me do that!

MRS. STONEHAY.

Oh, I see—I quite see. [*To* LESLIE.] How dare you tamper with my daughter — how dare you?

G

[*To* IRENE.] We will go home. You shall never
enter this house again ; our acquaintance with this
lady has terminated.

LESLIE.

Irene !

MRS. STONEHAY.

What ! Do you think by your mock-morality to
upset my calculations for Irene's welfare ? If so,
you can have this satisfaction for your pains—that
one word, one look, from me will do more with this
weak, ungrateful girl than a month of your impu-
dent meddling. Good morning.

[MRS. STONEHAY *and* IRENE *are going.*]

LESLIE.

Irene !

IRENE.

I—I told you I was a coward. Good-bye.

LESLIE.

Oh, Irene !

IRENE.

You have done your utmost to save me——!

LESLIE.

No! I have not yet done my utmost. Janet!
Janet !

[JANET *rises from the sofa with an effort, and*
LESLIE *takes her by the hand.*]

LESLIE.

Look here ! This poor child is a living sacrifice
to a man whose history is a horrible chapter of dis-
honour. He is a man who preys upon the weak un-

der the mask of a false name; who stabs but has not the mercy to kill; and who leaves his victims to bleed to death in their hearts, slowly but surely.

MRS. STONEHAY.

I always feared this was a worthless girl. But pray, what has her depravity to do with us?

LESLIE.

Only this. Janet has just discovered the whereabouts of the man she has been seeking.

MRS. STONEHAY.

Really this is no concern of ours.

LESLIE.

There you are mistaken, Mrs. Stonehay.

MRS. STONEHAY.

Mistaken?

LESLIE.

Yes. Because, if this man were willing to atone to Janet Preece by marrying her, he could not fulfil his engagement to your daughter.

IRENE.

Oh!

MRS. STONEHAY.

This is an infamous fabrication!

LESLIE.

[*To* JANET.] Is it the truth?

JANET PREECE.

It is—the truth.

[JANET *sinks back upon the sofa burying her face in the pillows.*]

IRENE.

Oh, Leslie!

MRS. STONEHAY.

A girl of that character lives upon her lying
romances, and the woman who harbours such a
creature becomes a partner and not a protector. [*To*
IRENE.] Come—do you hear me!

IRENE.

No, no! Leslie!

LESLIE.

Dunstan!

[DUNSTAN RENSHAW *and* LORD DANGARS *enter.*]

DUNSTAN RENSHAW.

[*Tenderly.*] Leslie. [*He bows to* MRS. STONEHAY
and IRENE.] Leslie, dear, let me introduce Lord
Dangars to you. [JANET *raises her head with a
startled look of horror.*]

LORD DANGARS.

[*Offering his hand.*] Mrs. Renshaw, I——

LESLIE.

No, Dunstan; forgive me—I cannot make the
acquaintance of Lord Dangars.

DUNSTAN RENSHAW.

[*In an undertone..*] Leslie!

LESLIE.

If Lord Dangars wishes for an explanation, Dun-

stan, I have only to recall to him the existence of this unhappy girl whose story is known to me.
[*She reveals* JANET.]

JANET PREECE.

No, no!

LESLIE.

Janet Preece.
[DUNSTAN *stares at* JANET *helplessly and horror-stricken.*]

LORD DANGARS.

I should not be so impolite as to disturb Mrs. Renshaw's prejudices against me were they founded upon less illusory evidence. But I can assure Mrs. Renshaw that I believe I have never seen this young lady until the present moment.
[LESLIE *looks aghast at* JANET.]

MRS. STONEHAY.

Janet, do *you* say you know Lord Dangars?

JANET PREECE.

No, no! It's not he I know! It is a mistake—I——

MRS. STONEHAY.

A mistake!

JANET PREECE.

Ah! Let me go! let me go!
[LESLIE *grasps her by the arm.*]

MRS. STONEHAY.

Girl, do you mean that you know *Mr. Renshaw?*
[DANGARS *and* LESLIE *turn to* DUNSTAN, *who is staring blankly before him with his hands clenched.*]

LESLIE.

Janet! Janet! [*As the truth dawns upon her.*] Oh!

JANET PREECE.

Ah! What have I done to you! I'd have died to save you this. God forgive me! I'm not fit to live! Kill me! Kill me! Ah!
    [*She rushes down the garden steps, past* LESLIE, *who is as one turned to stone.*]

MRS. STONEHAY.

Lord Dangars, may I trespass upon your good nature so far as to beg your escort home? Poor Irene is naturally much distressed.

LORD DANGARS.

[*Looking from* DUNSTAN *to* LESLIE.] This is perhaps not the time to express regrets——

MRS. STONEHAY.

Regrets! Regrets that the character of an honourable man is cleared from a gross and vindictive slander! It is not from *us* that regrets should come. I am ready.

IRENE.

[*Weeping.*] Leslie—Leslie! [*She takes* LESLIE'S *hand and kisses it.* LESLIE *stands, with staring eyes, immovable.*]

MRS. STONEHAY.

Irene, give your arm to Lord Dangars.
    [IRENE *gives her arm helplessly to* DANGARS. MRS. STONEHAY *shrugs her shoulders and goes out, followed by* DANGARS *with* IRENE.]

DUNSTAN RENSHAW.

[*In a hollow, changed voice.*] Leslie—Leslie! [*He staggers towards her.*] You hate me—you hate me. [*He looks into her face.*] How you hate me !

LESLIE.

[*Speaking with great effort.*] Deny it—deny it.

DUNSTAN RENSHAW.

Deny it !

LESLIE.

Deny it.

DUNSTAN RENSHAW.

I—I—Ah, God ! I'm guilty ! I'm guilty ! I'm guilty ! Don't ask me to tell you the story of my life—I can't—I can't. It's one of sin—all sin. Till I met you—till I met you. Can you hear me?
[*She nods her head twice, still with the wild dazed look in her face.*]

DUNSTAN RENSHAW.

Then everything altered. I love you—I love you ! In all the world there is nothing for me but you— you make my day or my night by the opening or the closing of your eyes. There is nothing for me but you ! I worship you !
[*The man is heard again singing to the mandolin.* LESLIE *shudders and tries to go.*]

DUNSTAN RENSHAW.

Don't leave me ! You won't leave me ! I can't live away from you. Have mercy on me ! Have mercy on me ! Mercy ! [*He kneels to her.*] I repent !

Help me to begin a new life! I'm young; I won't die till I've made amends. I won't die till I've done some good act to make you proud of me! Oh, give me hope!

LESLIE.

[*As if in a dream.*] Deny it!

DUNSTAN RENSHAW.

I'm guilty—you know it! Have mercy! Give me a faint hope! A year hence you'll pardon me? Two years—ten? A little hope—only a little hope!

LESLIE.

Deny it.

DUNSTAN RENSHAW.

I can't deny it!

LESLIE.

Go!

[*After a moment he goes quietly away, then she falls to the ground in a swoon. The voice of the singer rises in the distance.*]

END OF THE THIRD ACT.

THE FOURTH ACT.

THE BEGINNING OF A NEW LIFE.

The scene is HUGH MURRAY'S *private sitting-room in an old-fashioned Holborn hotel, comfortably and solidly furnished, but with an antiquated look about the place. It is evening, the lamps are lighted and the fire is burning.* HUGH *is playing a plaintive melody upon the piano, and watching* LESLIE, *who sits with a listless air.*

LESLIE.

Mr. Murray.

HUGH MURRAY.

Yes?

LESLIE.

Wilfrid is very late.

HUGH MURRAY.

He will be back soon.

LESLIE.

With the worn, hopeless look upon his face which makes my heart ache so. Do you guess why the poor boy is out and about from morning till night?

HUGH MURRAY.

Do I guess?

LESLIE.

Ah, you *do* guess. You know that my brother is searching for Janet Preece.

HUGH MURRAY.

Something of the kind has crossed my mind. Why does he look for her here?

LESLIE.

He ascertained that she left Florence before we hurried out of that dreadful city ; but she has not returned to her home in the country, and so he prays that the whirlpool has drawn her to London again and that he may find her.

HUGH MURRAY.

Does he confide in you?

LESLIE.

No, poor fellow—but I know, I know, I know. Oh, it's horrible that he can't forget her—horrible !

HUGH MURRAY.

Hush ! you must try not to think.

LESLIE.

I do try—I do try. How long have my brother and I been here? I can't reckon.

HUGH MURRAY.

You left Florence ten days ago ; you've been sharing an old bachelor's solitude almost a week.

LESLIE.

Dear friend, your solitude must be far better than such dismal company.

HUGH MURRAY.

Better ! No.

LESLIE.

Ah, yes. I wanted Wilfrid to be with me when I told you—but, I leave you early to-morrow.

HUGH MURRAY.

To-morrow !

LESLIE.

Yes. I've written to my old schoolmistress at Helmstead begging her to take me again—not to learn ; I've nothing more to learn ! But I want to sit amongst the girls again, to walk with them, and to run down to the brook with my hands in theirs as I did—only six weeks ago. Only six weeks ago.

HUGH MURRAY.

And Wilfrid ?

LESLIE.

Wilfrid has promised to visit me very often, as he used to. So everything will be as it was—just as it was.

HUGH MURRAY.

I knew you could not remain in this dreary hotel, but still—why so suddenly ?

LESLIE.

Because I've been thinking that if *he* should try to see me—you know whom I mean ?

HUGH MURRAY.

Yes.

LESLIE.

If he should try to see me again it is to you he would first come to ascertain my whereabouts.

Hugh Murray.

And surely you would grant him an interview?

Leslie.

Not yet! I'm not cruel—I used not to be cruel
—only I'm not ready to meet him yet.

Hugh Murray.

When will you be prepared to meet him?

Leslie.

How can I tell? I am like a dead woman dreaming after death. What good would it do him to look
upon a soulless woman!

Hugh Murray.

Is there no hope left for him?

Leslie.

Yes, a miracle —when there is hope for me.
[Wilfrid *enters, looking very weary and careworn.*]

Leslie.

Wilfrid dear.

Wilfrid Brudenell.

Well, Les.   [*He kisses her listlessly.*]

Hugh Murray.

You look fagged, my boy.

Wilfrid Brudenell.

Hallo, Murray. I am a bit done to-night.

Hugh Murray.

Walking?

Wilfrid Brudenell.

Flying like a blind bat, from one quarter of Lon-

don to another. I've got some business in hand, and
no one will do more than gape or laugh at a fellow
when he's in terrible earnest. This cursed city ! It
soaks up the poor and the helpless like a sponge ;
but I'll wring it dry yet—you'll see if I don't—
you'll see——

[*He twists the arm-chair round and sits facing the
fire.*]

LESLIE.

[*To* HUGH, *in a whisper.*] I told you so—he is
searching for her.

HUGH MURRAY.

Yes.

LESLIE.

What should I do if he found her !

HUGH MURRAY.

Nothing. Leave everything to chance.

LESLIE.

Chance !

HUGH MURRAY.

Chance is a fairer arbiter of our lives than we
imagine. You are terribly ill. [*She shakes her head.*]
I have written into the country for some fruit for
you ; it should have arrived by this time, with this
morning's bloom on it. I'll go and enquire. [*She
offers her hand, which he merely touches.*] Poor Will's
fast asleep. [*He goes out.*]

LESLIE.

[*Bending over* WILFRID.] Tired to death. Will,
my dear brother, you are the only one left me now

and you are drifting away from me. Your heart is no longer mine and your thoughts are no longer mine. It's so hard to lose husband and brother at once! Come back to me—come back to me!

[JANET, *looking very poor and ill, appears at the door.*]

LESLIE.

Oh! Janet!

JANET PREECE.

Mrs. Renshaw.

LESLIE.

How do you come here?

JANET PREECE.

I've been keeping near you since you left Florence. Days ago I found out you were here, through watching your brother and Mr. Murray. If I'd sent my name up to you you'd have refused to see me, so I've been waiting my opportunity to steal into the hotel while the porter was absent. Don't turn me away till you've heard me!

LESLIE.

Sit down, while I think for a moment.

JANET PREECE.

Thank you.

LESLIE.

[*To herself, looking at the arm-chair in which* WILFRID *is sleeping concealed from view.*] Chance has brought them together again and Mr. Murray says that chance is a just arbiter. I'll neither unite them nor keep them apart. Chance shall do everything for me. Well? Speak low, please.

JANET PREECE.

[*Pointing to door.*] Your brother is not in there?

LESLIE.

No. What do you want of me?

JANET PREECE.

To tell you this. I'm going out to Australia in company with some poor farming people from down near home ; I met them by chance here in London and it's settled. We sail from Plymouth the day after to-morrow, and there's an end o' me.

LESLIE.

Can I—do anything—to help you?

JANET PREECE.

Oh, no, no. But before I go I've got to ease my mind of something that you must listen to. It's this. I've parted you from your husband. Haven't I? Haven't I?

LESLIE.

Yes.

JANET PREECE.

Well, then, its only just to him that you should know this. It's *I* that tempted *him*, not he that led me on ; and I've lied to you in letting you think the man was to blame instead of the woman. I'm worthless, part of the rubbish of the world, and was so before I met him, and he's a better man than you think for. There!

LESLIE.

Janet, do you think I don't see through the falsehood you're telling me?

JANET PREECE.

The falsehood!

LESLIE.

You're trying to heal my sorrow with a fable. It's useless; I have heard the truth from my husband's lips.

JANET PREECE.

Ah, then, in pity for me, take him back! Don't let me go to my grave knowing that I've ruined your life for you. Try to blame me more! Try to blame me more!   [WILFRID *stirs in his sleep.*]

LESLIE.

Hush!

JANET PREECE.

We're not alone!

LESLIE.

My brother.

JANET PREECE.

[*In a whisper.*] He has not heard me. I'll go.

LESLIE.

Janet, I'll not keep the truth from you! Wilfrid loves you still.

JANET PREECE.

Oh, no!

LESLIE.

He has been searching for you for days past, and he is there now worn with trouble and anxiety for you.

JANET PREECE.

Oh, don't tell me! don't tell me!

LESLIE.

It would be a reproach to me if I let you go in ignorance; and now, Janet, I—I leave the rest to you.

JANET PREECE.

God bless you for the trust you place in me! You needn't fear me. Good-bye.

LESLIE.

Ah, Janet, I am so perplexed. We are both in trouble—both in trouble.

JANET PREECE.

In years to come, when I am only a mere speck in his life, you'll tell him, won't you ?

LESLIE.

Yes, yes.

JANET PREECE.

[*Irresolutely.*] You'll let me look at his face once more for the last time ? [LESLIE *nods her head. Looking at* WILFRID.] Good-bye. [*To* LESLIE.] He need never know.

> [*She slowly bends over* WILFRID *and kisses him upon the forehead. As she draws back behind the chair* WILFRID *opens his eyes and sees* LESLIE *standing before him.*]

WILFRID BRUDENELL.

Leslie, dear. I was dreaming and you woke me with your kiss. [JANET *steals out.*] What's that ? [HUGH *enters, carrying a basket of fruit.*] Oh, it's Murray.

H

LESLIE.

[*In an undertone to* HUGH.] Lend me some money
—some money. By-and-by I'll tell you why I want
it.

HUGH MURRAY.

[*To* LESLIE.] Gold or notes ?

LESLIE.

Either—both.
[*He hands her some money from a cabinet, and
she goes out.*]

HUGH MURRAY.

Wilfrid.

WILFRID BRUDENELL.

Yes ?

HUGH MURRAY.

Quick, man; before your sister returns ! I must
tell you. Renshaw is coming here to-night.

WILFRID BRUDENELL.

Renshaw !

HUGH MURRAY.

I received this note from him five minutes ago—a
few lines telling me he has returned to England and
entreating me to see him to-night.

WILFRID BRUDENELL.

You'll not meet him !

HUGH MURRAY.

Why not ? The man is suffering; I can read that
in his handwriting.

WILFRID BRUDENELL.

Suffering! Let him taste such suffering as he has dealt out to others. Is my sister not suffering? Is Janet Preece not suffering? Am I not suffering?

HUGH MURRAY.

Wilfrid, my boy, Wilfrid; there's something better to do than to be revenged.

WILFRID BRUDENELL.

How easy it is, Murray, for an onlooker to be charitable!

HUGH MURRAY.

Hush, my boy! Don't you see that there is no future for her except one of reconciliation with her husband?

WILFRID BRUDENELL.

Reconciliation!

HUGH MURRAY.

Her ideal is destroyed, her illusions are gone, but time will send Renshaw's sins further and further into the distance, and habit will teach her never to look back.

WILFRID BRUDENELL.

Murray, you don't know! You argue like a lawyer who has to patch up a mere wrangle between husband and wife.

HUGH MURRAY.

I don't know!

WILFRID BRUDENELL.

You don't know what it is to have the heart plucked out of you and trampled upon!

HUGH MURRAY.

Wilfrid, be silent!

WILFRID BRUDENELL.

How can you, living your level, humdrum life, gauge the penalty paid by those who love what is worth so much and yet so little! Ah, Murray, wait till you love and lose, as we have lost!

HUGH MURRAY.

Wait! [LESLIE *enters unnoticed.*] Wait! Do you think you can read me a lesson in despair? Come to me when your boy's passion has grown cold and I'll describe to you the agony of a man's hungry, hopeless, endless devotion.

WILFRID BRUDENELL.

Murray!

HUGH MURRAY.

I love your sister! I have loved her from the moment I first saw her in the school-garden at Helmstead; but I loved her too reverently to disturb the simplicity of her childhood, and I waited. I waited! Waited for him to scorch into her cheeks the first flame of consciousness—waited for her to make him her idol—waited for him to break her heart! Waited for this!

[*He sits with his face buried in his hands.*]

WILFRID BRUDENELL.

Murray—forgive me. I never thought of this. If we could have been brothers!

HUGH MURRAY.

Sssh! It is always as it is now, Will. Women

love men whose natures are like bright colours—the homespun of life repels them. They delight to hear their fate in the cadences of a musical voice, thinking they are listening to an impromptu ; it's too late when they learn that the melody has been composed by Experience and scored by other women's tears. [LESLIE *reveals herself.*]

WILFRID BRUDENELL.

My sister !

HUGH MURRAY.

Mrs. Renshaw ! I fear—you have heard.

LESLIE.

Yes.

HUGH MURRAY.

I never meant you to know ; I meant to carry it with me silently and patiently. The sorrow is mine —mine only.

LESLIE.

I — I can say nothing—nothing. Good-night. We will not meet to-morrow—I shall be gone early.

HUGH MURRAY.

Good-night.

LESLIE.

I shall never cease to pray for your good fortune. God bless you, Mr. Murray !

> [LESLIE *gives* HUGH *her hand, then she and* WIL-
> FRID *go out together. There is a knock at the
> door. A servant brings* HUGH *a card.*]

HUGH MURRAY.

Yes. [*The servant goes out.*]

HUGH MURRAY.

Renshaw.

[*The servant ushers in* DUNSTAN RENSHAW, *who looks broken and walks feebly.*]

DUNSTAN RENSHAW.

Speak to me, Murray.

HUGH MURRAY.

You look ill. Sit down.

DUNSTAN RENSHAW.

I have been ill, in Florence, and haven't had strength to struggle back to England till now.

HUGH MURRAY.

I'm sorry. What do you want of me?

DUNSTAN RENSHAW.

Friendship. If you're not my friend I haven't one in the world. Murray, you know where *she* is?

HUGH MURRAY.

Yes—I know.

DUNSTAN RENSHAW.

Tell me—tell me !

HUGH MURRAY.

I can't tell you. I—I may not tell you.

DUNSTAN RENSHAW.

Ah! I appeal to you. Exact any promise from me—be as hard on me as you please—only tell me, tell me ! [HUGH *is silent.*] Ah, you don't know what you're doing. I am mad. Night and day I see nothing but her face as it looked on me when she sent me from her ; night and day I hear nothing but that one word " Go," the last she spoke to me. The word won't let me sleep; it beats so on my brain. Another word, a simple message, from her might drive it out. Only tell me where she is ! My wife, Murray—my wife !

HUGH MURRAY.

I would tell you of my own will. But I can't break faith with her.

DUNSTAN RENSHAW.

She has not softened towards me then a little—a little, Murray ?

HUGH MURRAY.

Man, you must have patience.

DUNSTAN RENSHAW.

Patience !

HUGH MURRAY.

You must wait.

DUNSTAN RENSHAW.

Wait ! It is a hundred years since I lost her—a hundred years, and she has not softened towards me just a little.

[*He sits gazing vacantly upon the ground.*]

HUGH MURRAY.

[*To himself.*] Surely she would pity him if she saw him now, and if I can reconcile them it is my duty. I'll do my best; it will be my consolation

to have done my best. [*To* DUNSTAN.] Where are
you going when you leave me to-night?

DUNSTAN RENSHAW.

Let me rest here, in your room, for a few hours.

HUGH MURRAY.

Have you left your hotel?

DUNSTAN RENSHAW.

I am staying nowhere; I have been walking the
streets till I came here.

HUGH MURRAY.

I'll order you a room in this house.

DUNSTAN RENSHAW.

No, no. It's only here I can rest. I shall rest here.

HUGH MURRAY.

Why here?

DUNSTAN RENSHAW.

Because I shall feel sure that a friend's eyes will
look on me in the morning.

HUGH MURRAY.

Ring for what you want, otherwise the servants
won't disturb you.

DUNSTAN RENSHAW.

[*To himself.*] Won't disturb me—won't disturb
me. No.

HUGH MURRAY.

I'll leave you now. Good-night.

DUNSTAN RENSHAW.

You will not tell me where she is?

HUGH MURRAY.

Till I have her permission, I cannot.

DUNSTAN RENSHAW.

You mean that, guessing I should follow her, she has taken precautions to avoid me—to avoid me? Your face answers me.

HUGH MURRAY.

[*To himself.*] She will relent—I know she will relent.

DUNSTAN RENSHAW.

I shan't see you again to-night, Murray

HUGH MURRAY.

No—you'll not see *me*. Good night.

DUNSTAN RENSHAW.

Good-bye.

HUGH MURRAY.

[*To himself.*] But you shall see *her ;* I know she will relent. [*He goes out.*]

DUNSTAN RENSHAW.

Fool! fool! Why couldn't you have died in Florence? Why did you drag yourself all these miles—to end it *here?* I should have known better—I should have known better. [*He takes a phial from*

I

his pocket and slowly pours some poison into a tumbler.]
When I've proved that I could not live away from
her, perhaps she'll pity me. I shall never know it,
but perhaps she'll pity me then. [*About to drink.*]
Supposing I am blind ! Supposing there is some
chance of my regaining her. Regaining her! How dull
sleeplessness makes me ! How much could I regain
of what I've lost ! Why, *she knows me*—nothing can
ever undo that—*she knows me.* Every day would be
a dreary, hideous masquerade ; every night a wake-
ful, torturing retrospect. If she smiled, I should
whisper to myself—"yes, yes, that's a very pretty
pretence, but—*she knows you !* " The slamming of
a door would shout it, the creaking of a stair would
murmur it—"*she knows you !* " And when she
thought herself alone, or while she lay in her sleep,
I should be always steathily spying for that dreadful look upon her face, and I should find it again
and again as I see it now—the look which cries
out so plainly—"Profligate ! you taught one good
woman to believe in you, but now *she knows you !* "
No, no—no, no ! [*He drains the contents of the tumbler.*] The end—the end. [*Pointing towards the
clock.*] The hour at which we used to walk together
in the garden at Florence—husband and wife—
lovers. [*He pulls up the window-blind and looks out.*]
The sky—the last time—the sky. [*He rests drowsily
against the piano.*] Tired—tired. [*He walks rather
unsteadily to the table.*] A line to Murray. [*Writing.*] A line to Murray—telling him—poison—mor-
phine—message—— [*The pen falls from his hand
and his head drops forward.*] The light is going out.
I can't see. Light—I'll finish this when I wake—
I'll rest. [*He staggers to the sofa and falls upon it.*]

I shall sleep to-night. The voice has gone. Leslie —wife—reconciled——

[LESLIE *enters softly and kneels by his side.*]

LESLIE.

Dunstan, I am here. [*He partly opens his eyes, raises himself, and stares at her; then his head falls back quietly.* LESLIE's *face averted.*] Dunstan, I have returned to you. We are one and we will make atonement for the past together. I will be your Wife, not your Judge—let us from this moment begin the new life you spoke of. Dunstan! [*She sees the paper which has fallen from his hand, and reads it.*] Dunstan! Dunstan! No, no! Look at me! Ah! [*She catches him in her arms.*] Husband! Husband! Husband!

THE END.

www.ingramcontent.com/pod-product-compliance
Lightning Source LLC
Chambersburg PA
CBHW021136020726
47500CB00003B/1102